SARAH'S STORY

Mollie Hardwick

Against the background of music-halls and
saloons, East End sweatshops and mission
halls, SARAH'S STORY tells of a young
girl's struggle for survival above and below
the poverty line in late Victorian London.

With the cheek, good humour and sharpness
of a Cockney waif, Sarah copes with every
pitfall that awaits an orphaned girl of 13 and
emerges unscathed from her encounters with
the sharks and charlatans who seek to
exploit her.

Mollie Hardwick's moving and evocative
portrait of London low life at the turn of the
century ends as Sarah decides to go into
domestic service below stairs in the Bellamy
household at 165 Eaton Place.

Sarah's Story

MOLLIE HARDWICK

SPHERE BOOKS LIMITED
30/32 Gray's Inn Road, London WC1X 8JL

First published in Great Britain by Sphere Books Ltd 1973
Published by arrangement with Sagitta Productions Ltd
Copyright © Sagitta Productions Ltd 1973
Reprinted 1973, 1974, 1976, 1978

TRADE
MARK

Set in Times Roman

Printed in Great Britain by
Hazell Watson & Viney Ltd
Aylesbury, Bucks

BOOK ONE: PRELUDE TO CLEMENCE

CHAPTER ONE

'The hell with omnibuses!' she said aloud, to the horror of a passing old lady, and marched briskly to a cab standing at the station rank.

'Where to, miss?'

'Belgravia,' she said grandly, adding in an execrable pidgin-French accent. 'I do not read ze English well. Drive me to zis address,' and she handed the scribbled-on envelope to the surprised driver. 'A rum-un,' he thought, 'but it takes all sorts. Righto, Mamzell,' he said aloud, and with a flick of the whip the cab was on its way westwards. Clemence leaned back in her seat and waved regally to imaginary crowds, as she had seen the beautiful Queen Alexandra acknowledge the homage of her people.

Half an hour later, outwardly cool and cocky, inwardly taut with nervous excitement, Clemence was ringing the front-door bell of 165 Eaton Place, the home of Richard Bellamy, M.P., and his wife Lady Marjorie. Soon she would be Clemence no more. On the other side of the area door, to which Mr. Hudson the butler would very properly direct her, she would be transformed into Sarah.

It had all begun 24 years earlier.

Marianne rubbed her hands together inside her small muff. It was getting colder and colder. The sky over Islington changed colour, from purple to the orange-pink glow of an autumn sunset, outlining the twisted London chimneys, black silhouettes from which came little trails of smoke as evening fires were lit. Soon the splendid, flauntingly modern for 1879, electric lamps at the gates of the Theatre Royal, New Sadler's Wells, would spring into life, a sign that the crowd milling round the gates was about to be let in.

It *was* chilly. Marianne wished she had put on her cloak, but her dress was her very best; she'd only finished it the night before, specially for the opening of the rebuilt playhouse. Thoughtfully, she eyed a coffee stall, where a shawled woman was dispensing steaming cups from a metal vat. Would it be 'fast' to go and buy one? If only she had a gentleman friend to bring it to her! But there was nobody, only Elsie from the milliner's where they both worked, and Elsie wasn't here yet. Her old mother was probably ill again. At least, Marianne reflected, her own mother was still young. She advanced to the coffee stall and produced a penny from the small change she kept in her glove.

The coffee was thin and poor, but deliciously hot. Marianne drank eagerly. Almost half the cup was gone when a sudden jolting of her elbow sent the other half flying, some falling in a hot cascade on the ground and the rest, oh horror, on the skirt of her new dress. Angrily she spun round.

'Why don't you look where you're going, clumsy?'

The young man who had caused the accident blushed to the curly brim of his bowler.

'I say, I'm awfully sorry, Miss! Have I gone and spoilt your frock? I don't know how it happened, I don't really.'

Marianne was dabbing at the wet patch on her best merino.

'Good thing it's brown,' she said. 'Now if it'd been *hers* over there', nodding towards a dowager in lilac velvet, 'I bet you'd have got a telling off!' They both laughed.

'What about me buying you another cup?'

'I won't say no.'

The boy produced some money, rattling it with pride, and bought coffee for her and for himself. His blush was fading. Marianne, sipping in a ladylike manner, eyed him covertly through her long lashes. He was nineteen or twenty, she guessed, splendidly built, with the broad shoulders and narrow hips of a boxer. His high-buttoned jacket was sailor blue, matching his eyes, his brown hair curly, his features aquiline and well-cut. He reminded Marianne of William, the hero of *Black-eyed Susan*, at the Surrey Theatre. She decided to smile at him.

To be at the receiving end of Marianne's smile was worth a good deal more than the price of a cup of coffee. Two lustrous dark eyes beamed at him from a face rosy with the cold.

Her hair was dark, like her eyes, a curly foam of fringe beneath the fashionable Dolly Varden hat, the netted chignon behind resting against a white neck. Brown eyes, brown hair, a brown dress, tight to the figure all the way down to the knees, then flaring out, giving her the appearance of having a mermaid's tail, if one could imagine a mermaid with distracting little pearl buttons from neck to hem. His gaze settled below the neck, and he was glad she had not bothered to put on a cloak, for beneath their thin woollen covering her breasts were two entrancing peaks, which might as well have been naked, so clearly outlined were they.

'Hope you'll know me again,' she said.

'I hope I'll see you again.'

'Saucy.'

'No, straight, I mean it. Tell us your name.'

'Why not? It's Marianne Dumas, and I work for Madame Billings the milliner, her address being 128 High Street, Islington. Anything else?'

'Dumas. That's French, isn't it?'

Her head tilted proudly. 'My grandfather was the great French writer, Alexandre Dumas, and he wrote books that get read all over the world. I've read some of them. Well, bits.'

His eyes were wide. 'Go on! Can you speak French, then? I've never met anyone that spoke French.'

'Not really. My Pa died when I was only a little thing, and Ma was English, so I never learned to speak it proper. I can say the words like they do in France, though, and I can sing French songs, because Pa was musical. He played the fiddle in the orchestra at the Grand Theatre, and he used to teach me all sorts of songs. Then I went to work at the

7

Convent as a sewing-maid, and the nuns used to say I sang beautiful. Beautifully,' she corrected hastily, remembering various sharp nips and slaps she had received from Sister Agatha for the backslidings in grammar.

'A theatre orchestra! Lor. I've never met anyone from a theatre, for all that I spend every bit of money I earn on 'em. That's why I came here tonight, for the Grand Opening . . .'

The Grand Opening! They stared at each other. The coffee-stall proprietor was gone. The tail-end of the crowd which had surrounded them could be seen filing into the theatre doors, and on the gate-posts the electric lamps were blazing. They had heard nothing, seen nothing, rapt in the enchantment of their first meeting. He put his hand on her arm.

'Time we went in,' he said. Their eyes locked in that mutual gaze which is a signal-light. She tucked her hand into the crook of his arm, and they moved towards Sadler's Wells Theatre, rebuilt and vastly improved, about to present the musical drama *Rob Roy*, under the new management of the enterprising American, Mr. Bateman. The entrance-hall displayed smart pomegranate-patterned wallpaper, designed by William Morris, warmed by a blazing fire in a central grate; the orchestra was tuning up, refreshment-sellers hawked their wares. The act-drop showing the old Wells Spa rose portentously, to reveal electric-blue curtains, and majestic Mrs. Bateman, her ample form draped in the tartan robes of Helen MacGregor, delivering a poetic prologue about the theatre's past splendours, the nights of tragic Kean and the clown Grimaldi with his monkey-baby face, of John Braham who had sung for Nelson's Emma. For all this, Marianne's escort had paid two shillings each for their seats; dutifully they watched and listened, but in the darkness their heads turned towards each other and their hands stole together. Their own drama was beginning: *Rob Roy* stood no chance.

In fact, it stood very little with the rest of that critical first-night audience, the cheaper parts of the house ever

8

ready to offer helpful comments or suggestions to the actors. The hero, Francis Osbaldistone, they addressed as Baldy within a few minutes of the rising of the curtain, and interrupted him during a long sentimental duologue with the heroine with a request to 'Cut the cackle and come to the 'osses', while the aristocratic Sir Frederick, obviously suffering from a bad cold, was offered 'the loan of a wipe'. The tedium of the first act was fortunately relieved by the opening of the second, described in the programme as 'Loch Lomond by Moonlight', but in fact presenting every appearance of being a solicitor's office. When the delighted gallery had roared itself hoarse over this blunder it was in time to make some general remarks about Rob Roy's kilt and sporran, which caused Marianne to turn her blushing face away from her companion. By the time the famous fight was reached and the claymore of The Dougal of Dougal was clashing against the rapier of Captain Thornton, the gallery-ites and pittites were prepared to enjoy anything, the pleasures of the drama being enhanced by those of shrimps, oranges and bottled beer.

When the manly figure of Mr. Bentley, as Rob Roy, stepped forward to conclude the act with a rousing musical summons to his clan, the audience helpfully joined in:

'Our signal for fight, which from monarchs we drew,
 Must be heard but by night in our vengeful halloo!'

he bellowed, to be echoed from the gallery in a lusty hunting-chorus of 'Yoicks!' 'Gone away!' and 'Tally-ho!' and his final assertion that while there were leaves in the forest, and foam on the river, MacGregor, despite them, should flourish for ever, drew encouraging cries of 'That's right, me bhoy! Never say die, old cock!' and a patriotic roar of 'The Russians shall not have Constantin-o-ople!'

As the curtain descended on the perspiring Mr. Bentley and the house lights went up the two watchers in the pit drew away from each other. Marianne had taken off her hat, as ladies were expected to do in the theatre, and her companion gazed admiringly at her rich uncovered hair. She caught his look, and said hastily:

9

'Lovely, isn't it!'

'Ain't it just, though!'

'Silly.' She patted it complacently. '*Ought* to be curly, of course. My great-great-grandma was coloured.'

'Go on! Christy Minstrel, was she?'

She gave his arm a mock-exasperated push. 'Oh, you're ridiculous. She was a West Indian, sort of coffee-colour. Anyway, what are we talking about my hair for? I meant the play was lovely. Or don't you like it?'

'What I can hear of it for the row up there. Shouldn't think they'll give 'em the bird, though. You can tell they're good-tempered.'

She looked at him inquisitively. 'Know a lot about it, don't you? Ought to be on the stage yourself.'

He shook his head. 'Not much chance of that. I'm a law clerk. Likely to stay one.'

'Here,' she said suddenly. 'I don't even know your name, do I?'

'Albert Moffat, at your service. Named after the late lamented Prince Consort, previous to 'is untimely decease which prevented 'im 'aving the pleasure of knowing me.'

As she giggled, he raised her to her feet. 'Come on, let's partake of some refreshments, as it might be jellied eels, while admiring the beauties of this 'andsome auditorium.'

Marianne looked round at the splendours on every side, the dazzling electric chandelier, the crimson of Phipps' Patent Theatre Chairs, the sky-blue and gold paint, the classical figures of nymphs and shepherds paying homage to a girlish Queen Victoria above the proscenium arch. It was the biggest, the most modern theatre in London.

The play was over. The Family Circle had wrapped up itself and its children in coats, bonnets and mufflers and gone to its several domestic hearths, while the Balcony Stalls and Private Boxes, cloaked, furred and top-hatted, had been conducted to their hansoms and private carriages; the pit and gallery, loud in discussion of the performance, had straggled away through the Islington streets, some to the

10

Angel round the corner, others to the Shakespeare's Head and the Clown that nestled in the shadow of the theatre. Albert drew Marianne towards the open door of the Shakespeare's Head, a cavern of bright light and smoke.

'Come on, let's wash down the eels.'

Marianne looked with distaste at the drinkers within.

'All right. But not for long, mind.'

Albert ushered her into the crowded saloon, and by sleight-of-hand whipped a stool from beneath a man who was just going to sit on it, and ensconced Marianne in a corner. 'Wines, spirits, beers and cyders as supplied to all the crowned 'eads of Europe, expense no object.' Marianne pulled a face. 'No, thank *you*! I'll have lemonade, please. Sweet.'

It seemed only a moment before he was back with a glass for her and another for himself. 'My! that was quick,' she said. He struck a Tuppence Coloured attitude. 'Harlequin Moffat, that's me. The quickness of the 'and deceives the eye.' Her glass half-way to her lips, she stopped and looked at him. 'That's not lemonade, is it?'

'If it is, the barman ain't up to 'is job, 'cause I ordered brandy.'

'Brandy! That's a strong, nasty drink.'

'Strong it may be, but nasty . . . well, some might say it was.'

'Then why do you drink it?' she challenged.

Albert shrugged. 'Puts a bit of shine on life, you might say. Drink up, now. To us.' His glass touched hers with a musical clink.

She refused a second drink, saying that the heat made her giddy and the fumes were unpleasant. 'Besides,' she added, 'people are looking at me. I don't think you ought to have brought me in here. Please take me home.'

They walked slowly through the streets and squares between the Wells and the house where, she told him, she lived with her mother, who worked as a shop-assistant in Jay's drapery store, Regent Circus. Mama seldom got home before eleven at night, tired out with standing; Marianne liked

11

to be home first to have a little supper waiting for her.

They said little as they walked. In his mind was a confused sensation of having found something precious which he had no right to claim. In his twenty years of life he had known few women other than his married sister and her friends. No females were employed in the legal firm where he worked, in shabby, cold offices high above the green of Gray's Inn Gardens. Since he had been old enough to notice feminine charms his fancy had been caught by one actress or ballet-girl after another, etherealised, unobtainable creatures in frothy spangled skirts, glittering as their paste jewels and as delusive. Many a night, after the play, he had mustered up the courage to wait for one of them outside the stage door; had seen by the flickering gas-lamp his goddess emerge, bonneted and shawled, traces of paint still about her long mysterious eyes and on her lips. Sometimes he had spoken; once he had presented a bunch of violets bought earlier, drooping from the warmth of his pocket, and had received a mechanical smile and a curt 'Thanks.' At other times his tentative overtures would be received with giggles, and the young lady would flit past him in a waft of Jockey Club perfume, to be swallowed up by the foggy night. Once he had even had his face slapped. It seemed that good looks got you nowhere with theatrical ladies. If they were virtuous they were in haste to go home to their families; if they were not, a young man in a suit shiny with wear stood not a chance. 'A Piccadilly masher,' Albert had thought gloomily, 'that's what I oughter be.' He had become a little disillusioned, aware that they were never quite so pretty off the stage as on it. Yet no 'real girl', as he thought of them, had charmed him as much. They wore no make-up to transform their faces into rosy pearls, more often than not their complexions were sallow and even grime-ingrained by London smoke, their teeth bad and their noses red from frequent draughts of scalding hot tea.

And now this luminary had risen in his skies, the sensible part of his nature told him that he was too young and too poor to marry, and that on no other terms would Miss Marianne Dumas be available. Her virtue was proclaimed in her clear eyes, in the gentle touch of her arm against his, in her distaste for drink, in her frank but modest turn of wrist and ankle. No scuffles in dark alleys for Miss Dumas. Not that Albert knew much about such encounters, for like so many young Victorians of his class he was still virgin at twenty.

No, he was caught all right, whether he liked it or not. He was not quite sure that he did like it, for all the rapturous sensations born in him by the warmth of her at his side and the sound of her pretty voice.

'I wouldn't like to come down to that,' she was saying. She had paused at the area-railings of a house in which, framed in the lighted basement window, a white-capped head was bent over a stone sink. The window was barred, the head, whose owner was obviously washing up, seemed bowed in subjection like that of a captive animal.

'I wouldn't be in service for anything,' Marianne went on. 'Slaving away at dirty jobs for people that'd look down their noses at you. No freedom, no nothing.' She glanced up mischievously. 'And no followers – that's what they say!'

'I'd like to see 'em keep *me* out,' replied Albert gallantly. If he was doomed he might as well rush on his fate. 'Take a regiment of Life Guards to do that.' A tiny squeeze of his arm was his reward. They had reached the Pentonville Road; her home, she said, was in White Lion Street, near her place of work. As they passed St. James's Church Albert held her tighter and quickened his pace, having been told that females were inclined to shudder in the vicinity of graveyards. But Marianne paused and looked back. 'I wonder what *he* was up to,' she said.

'Who?'

'That man – in the churchyard.'

Several things a man might be up to in a churchyard occurred to Albert, but he forbore to point them out. He followed her gaze. The church, a pale mass, rose above the shadowed grass and dim shapes of grave-stones, half-seen in starlight and the faint beams from a street-lamp. He saw no sign of life, and said so.

13

'But he's there . . . no, he isn't, he's gone now.'

'Nipped inside to swipe the candlesticks, I shouldn't wonder.'

'Oh no, he didn't look that kind of man a bit. More like . . . well, he looked sad and jolly at the same time. Funny, I could swear I seen him before, somewhere. It was his eyes, I think, very big and black, and he had a lot of white round his neck; some sort of collar.'

Albert gently urged her on. 'It was a gravestone you saw, I reckon, or the shadows. They make funny pictures, specially when you're tired.'

'I'm *not* tired, and I did see him. Anyway, he saw us, I know he did.'

They had reached her door; the unpretentious old house that held, she told him, three families beside herself and her mother. There was a faint yellow light in the window she pointed out as theirs.

'Mama's home,' she said. 'I've got to go in.'

They stood fronting each other, touching hands. For some reason he didn't kiss her; and she, for some reason, was glad.

'Good-night. And thank you for a lovely time, Mr Moffat.'

'Thank *you*, Miss Dumas. Can I see you again, please?'

She pretended to consider. 'You can call Sunday morning, if you like.'

Then she was gone, and the door shut behind her.

In the splendid hall of the new Sadler's Wells the portrait of Joseph Grimaldi, greatest and most tragic of clowns, looked down with dark Italian eyes on what they had made of his theatre, the old playhouse where he had clowned and danced, and sung and suffered. His body rested now in the churchyard in Pentonville Road; his spirit, it was said, lingered about the scenes of his earthly life.

CHAPTER TWO

'Ow Lord, my feet!' groaned Harriet Dumas, easing herself out of a worn laced-up boot. 'They get worse every blessed day. Why we shop-girls aren't allowed to sit down, when the good God gave us bottoms, I don't know.'

Mrs. Dumas relaxed thankfully in the basket chair. Slighter than Marianne, with fairer colouring, her expressions were sometimes startlingly similar, giving her the look of a faded pastel beside a glowing portrait in oils. She was thirty-eight, and though years of hard work to bring up her child single-handed and support them both had drawn lines of tiredness on her face and strewn pepper-and-salt streaks in her auburn hair, she was still appealingly pretty. Cockney resilience had always come to her rescue when things were blackest; even when her young husband had coughed himself to death. She had put no other man in his place, these ten years. The leers and hand-pressures which often came her way across the shop-counter she dismissed with a toss of her head as Blessed Cheek.

'Any vile seducers today, Mama?' Marianne enquired over her shoulder as she warmed the teapot.

'Let's see . . . yes, two. An old gent with one foot in the grave; couldn't hardly get up the strength to wink at me. And a flash chap with a monocle and a fish-faced wife.'

'Not much of a catch, then. But you wait till the Duke comes along.'

'Ah, His Grace!' She fluttered her eyelashes and an imaginary fan. 'Ho, really, Your Grace, Ai don't quaite know if Ai wish to accept your proffered *h*and. Seven castles is a lot to run, and Ai *h*ave *h*eard you're terribly under-staffed . . . Come on, where's that tea? I'm parched.'

'Ready if you are.'

They sat down to a supper that might not have done for His Grace but to them was richness; a pair of kippers, bread

15

with a thin spreading of treasured butter, and two baked apples, cheap and tasty. Marianne's young appetite had been barely touched by the jellied eels.

Marianne embarked on the story of her evening, omitting the episode of the Shakespeare's Head.

'H'm.' Mrs. Dumas eyed her daughter's heightened colour and fingers plaiting the tablecloth fringe. 'You seem very struck with the young man.'

'Oh, I know what you're thinking, Mama, but he's not like that. He never tried anything on – never touched me only for taking me arm.'

Mrs. Dumas's face was sad, remembering. 'Yes. It was like that with me and your father. I was quite surprised, after all I'd heard about Frenchmen.' She giggled. 'A bit disappointed, really. So he walked you home and nothing happened.'

'Oh – I'd forgotten. There was one thing . . .'

She recounted the curious incident of the man in the churchyard. 'But it's hardly worth telling. Mr. Moffat said it was only a shadow. I expect it was, now I think about it.'

She cleared the table and washed the supper pots in the stand-basin which also served for their own ablutions. Every morning it and the kettle were filled from the tap in the basement used by all the tenants, and every night it was laboriously carried downstairs with the slops to be emptied into the drain. It never occurred to Mrs. Dumas to regard this system as inconvenient. Only in private houses were water-tanks, wash-basins and baths connected to drains to be found; the empty-it-yourself type was taken for granted in lodging-houses, as was the shared commode in the back yard. No landlord could be expected to supply his tenants with fancy fittings for the twelve shillings a week they paid him.

She would have liked something a bit more stylish, but who wouldn't? They were perfectly comfortable with the landlord's shabby furniture and the touches of feminine taste they had introduced themselves; a red velvet drape fringed with bobbles for the mantelpiece, a vase of silk flowers brought home by Marianne from Madame Billings's workroom rejects, a coloured print of Her Majesty in girlhood, smiling brightly in Coronation robes, a Staffordshire figure of Disraeli, another of Kean as Richard III recoiling from his nightmare vision. The violin which had belonged to Julien Dumas was lovingly displayed on a wall.

The china put away, she stood gazing at the dissolving pictures in the dying fire. Marianne's dark-eyed gentleman in the churchyard of St. James's had been, she knew, no illusion. As a little girl, Marianne had seen things no one else could see. She had never been scolded for telling fibs, for her parents knew she was not lying when she said that a pretty lady 'with white hair, all up on top of her head, only she didn't look any older than you, Mama', had come and looked at her in bed during the night, or that a little boy had wandered through the room, dragging a toy horse on a string, and 'gone out through the wall.' Since adolescence Marianne seemed to have lost her clairvoyance. Now, her mother thought with a pang, it had come back for a reason; her child was a woman in love, with senses sharpened to receive not only the electric vibrations of sex, but the impressions still hanging on the air of an old room, or above a grave.

She made a decision. 'My dear, this gentleman of yours –'

Marianne was taking off her apron: 'Mr. Moffat?'

'No, the one in the churchyard. You may not remember it, my dear, but you always could see things we couldn't. Your Papa knew why, for he could too, and his Papa before him. Clairvoyance, they called it – French for seeing clear. It came right down from your Papa's grandma.'

'The black lady?'

'Marie-Cessette Dumas. She was as pretty as a picture, black though she was, your Papa remembered his Papa saying, the only time he ever came to see him; and whether she was properly married to your great-grandpa or not she thought she was, and *he* was a Count, Count Alexandre Davy de la Pailleterie. (There, I've said it right.)'

Marianne's face was troubled. 'But what *is* it, Mama?'

'Well, the way I've heard it, she was a sort of young witch.

17

They have this magic in Haiti, where she was born. Voodoo, they call it, and some pretty queer goings-on they get up to, if you ask me. I – if you like I'll show you something that belonged to her.'

She went to the chest of drawers and delved among linens. When she came back to the table she was holding a small package, wrapped in delicate silk shot with lights of green and gold.

'This is it. Be careful, it's very old.'

She watched silently as Marianne unwound the covering. Inside was a doll, twelve inches or so long. It represented a woman, her cotton skin black as night. Bright eyes stared out, darker from the dazzle of their surrounding whites; the mouth was a gash of scarlet. The doll wore a dress of many colours, tight-waisted and full-skirted, in the style of the early eighteenth century; a yellowed lace fichu draped its shoulders, on its head was a marvellous turban of green and scarlet silk worked with imitation jewels and tiny feathers. Marianne lifted a corner of it.

'It's got real hair!'

Her mother nodded. 'Look at – the rest of it.' Marianne slipped down the fichu from the smooth black shoulders. The doll had perfect miniature breasts, tipped with brown-aureoled scarlet nipples. Marianne gasped. 'Go on, lift the skirt,' said her mother.

Beneath the full skirt was a cambric petticoat. Beneath that the doll had the form of a complete woman, a triangle of black hair between voluptuous black thighs. And not only the hair on the head was real.

Fascinated, repelled, Marianne lifted one of the hands. The tiny fingers were tipped with what were unmistakable fragments of human nails. She dropped it as though it were red-hot.

'Oh, Mama, get rid of it! Throw it out!'

'I can't, love. Because it belonged to your Papa's family. I've so little of him left . . .'

Marianne was still staring at the doll. 'But what *is* it? Why . . .'

18

'It's a love-charm doll. Aida Weydo, the Black Venus. They used to have 'em made when they wanted to make a person fall in love, and then get some of the person's hair and nails and put them on the doll and then they could work charms over it.'

Marianne rewrapped the doll and handed it back. 'Put it away, do. I wish I hadn't seen it.'

Harriet patted her shoulder. 'I only showed it you because it's part of this thing, this magic that you've got yourself. None of us can help what we've got in our blood; I just don't want you to be frightened if you see anything else like your gentleman last night. It's like – like –' her townswoman's mind sought for a simile – 'like owls being able to see the wind.'

Marianne's gloom dissolved. 'That's pigs, Mama, not owls!'

'Is it, love? Well, anyway, there it is. Don't worry – you'll forget about it.'

And, oddly enough, Marianne did.

Albert called to pay his respects on the following Sunday morning.

His parents viewed his departure with the resigned disapproval that marked most of their reactions to their son's doings. His father, a bank teller, had from boyhood been a devout member of Woodbridge Chapel, Clerkenwell, a stubbornly Independent place of worship, whose membership rule was that 'every candidate do satisfy our minister as to his or her spiritual state. We hold and proclaim the distinctive doctrines of grace, as recorded in the 17th Article of the Church of England.' William Moffat came of a Scots family; Covenanting ancestors of his had positively enjoyed being martyred for their faith, one Farmer Moffat ending up nailed to his own barn door by Royalist soldiers infuriated by his rhetoric. William Moffat failed to understand why his younger son (the elder had run away to sea at the age of fourteen) should prefer to moon about wicked playhouses rather than study the Scriptures. He regarded the neatly-dressed Albert, solicitously brushing his bowler hat in the lobby.

'Going out on the Devil's business again?' he enquired, sourly.

'That's right, Father,' Albert replied cheerfully, 'Keeps me nicely in pin-money, runnin' errands for Old Nick.'

'Don't be impertinent! And I'll thank you not to joke on sacred subjects, particularly on the Lord's Day.' Mr. Moffat's accent grew thicker when provoked. His wife, sensing an impending sermon, emerged from the sitting-room. She had once been a pretty girl with a ready laugh, but life with William had cured her of a taste for what he called fal-lals and frivolities. Now, in the plain black bonnet and cloak which were her best Sunday wear, she looked as old as he did. Peace at any price, was her motto. She laid a tiny hand, like a mole's paw, on the arm raised in denunciation.

'We'll be late for Meeting, Will.'

'Aye. I'm ready.' He glowered at his son. 'I suppose ye'll no' see the Light and accompany us to Meeting?'

'Well, you might say I'm going to a meetin' meself, Father – not your sort, though. Ta-ta!' Blowing a kiss to his mother, he let himself out of the little house where there was no laughter, and made briskly up Rosoman Street towards Pentonville, that blessed district which had the unspeakable honour of housing his love, singing, as he went, the beautiful and pathetic strains of *Weeping, Sad and Lonely*, varying somewhat the original words.

'Take this sausage to my mother,
    Tell her that it comes from me;
If she asks you what it's made of,
    Tell her it's a mysteree.'

Singing to keep your pecker up, me laddo, he told himself. For all his elation he was as nervous as a kitten. Perhaps the night at the Wells had been all moonshine, beglamoured with theatre magic (though magic had been conspicuous by its absence from *Rob Roy*, come to think of it). Perhaps he ought not even to be thinking of courting seriously on his meagre seventeen shillings a week, seven-and-six of which he gave his mother for his keep. Perhaps Marianne's mother would object to him on sight. Perhaps Marianne would be disappointed in his appearance by daylight; he felt his chin, conscious of a few lingering adolescent spots. Perhaps . . .

But of course he might have saved himself the trouble of worrying. In White Lion Street he was received with warmth by Harriet, maternal and coquettish by turns, suffering a tiny rueful pang of jealousy that her child should have captured this handsome boy. And Marianne, more beautiful than ever in the morning sunshine that a seventeen-year-old complexion could face fearlessly, gave him her small hand with its roughened fingertips, and let it lie clasped in his own, for more than a handshake's length. The shabby room was an enchanted palace. He received formal permission to Walk Out with Marianne.

That winter of heavy rain, morasses of mud, and death-laden yellow London fogs might have been an Antipodean summer, for all the lovers knew. At Christmas came the pantomime, the old delights of Joey the Clown, called after the long-dead Grimaldi, the Columbine and attendant fairies whose simpers and spangles were no longer any allurement to Albert. And after the calendar turned to the year 1880, they saw for a few pence the gods of the Lyceum, the great Irving, a hump-backed spidery Richard III to the mournful beauty of Ellen Terry, Lady Anne, a vision of cloudy golden hair and diaphanous black robes. At the Egyptian Hall in Piccadilly, 'England's Home of Mystery', they thrilled and gasped to the wonders of Maskelyne and Cooke the illusionists. Was there ever a more perfect excuse for a girl to clutch her companion's arm and shrink close to him than the remarkable spectacle of Mr. Cooke's being beheaded by Mr. Maskelyne, 'in an easy and pleasant manner', provoking shrieks of laughter as the victim replaced the head on his neck? At the St. James's Hall, on the other side of Piccadilly, the Moore and Burgess Minstrels provided mirth and melody, the sad and exultant songs of the American Civil

War, the wistful ballads of Stephen Foster, at whose tenderer passages Albert's arm would steal round Marianne's eighteen-inch waist. It cost a shilling each to sit in the most comfortable gallery in London, but where else could lovers go on a winter night? Not to her home, for propriety's sake; not to his, for he had not yet dared to mention his courtship there.

With Spring there came the pleasures of Rosherville Gardens; a sail down to Gravesend, only sixpence each to go in. There they could dance till eleven at night to the music of a band, admire the plants in the great conservatory, pity the shabby captive bears in their pit, morosely catching the stale buns tossed to them by trippers, or consume tea and shrimps in the Baronial Hall.

How delightful was that Spring! After his long day in the stale chilliness of Raymond Buildings, hers in the airless chatter-filled workroom of Madame Billings, stitching away at pretty bonnets some other head would wear, it was bliss itself to meet in the evening and take the twopenny tram to Highgate Archway. There they would alight and stroll, arm-in-arm, past the Whittington Stone, up the steep hill that broke the hearts of coach-horses to the little village at the top. Every other building seemed to be an inn. The Crown, the Duke's Head, the Prince of Wales, the Angel, the Red Lion; nineteen in all, their swinging sign-boards called to Albert like resistless sirens. It was at the Red Lion and Sun that they had their first quarrel.

'I don't want to go in, Albert,' Marianne said for the third time. 'I don't like such places, you know that. And I'm not thirsty.'

'Well, I *am*!' he snapped back. 'I ain't walked all this perishing way to do without a drink when I get 'ere.'

Woman-like, she changed course to wound him. 'Why don't you watch your h's? You talk really common when you're vexed.'

He rose to the bait. 'Talk common, do I? Ever heard yourself on the phonograph?'

'No, I haven't, but I should hope I'd sound better than you!'

'My Gawd, *women*!'

'And don't you swear at me, Albert Moffat.'

'I'll swear if I want to, and I'll drop me h's if I want to, and I'll 'ave a drink if I want to, and you can – you can walk 'ome by yourself.'

'Thank you, I'm sure, Mr. Moffat,' she returned with exaggerated refinement. 'That's just what I'm going to do.'

They glared at each other. Marianne tossed her head, turned her back on him, and marched smartly away down the road, the way they had come. Swearing to himself, Albert pushed his way into the tavern. His pint of old-and-mild tasted sour; he gulped it without enjoyment. Serve her right, the bad-tempered cat. She'd soon get tired of walking. If he stayed in the pub long enough she'd be back, sure enough.

But she didn't appear. Time after time the door opened; it was never her. Suddenly Albert dashed his unfinished pint down on to the counter and strode out, followed by the mildly wondering eyes of several villagers.

He caught up with her half-way down Highgate Hill, still marching gamely though handicapped by her hobble skirt and tight best shoes. She heard his running steps but pretended not to hear them. When he reached her, panting, she half-turned her head for a contemptuous glance and walked on. He threw an arm round her.

'Love, I'm sorry! I'm sorry! I'm a beastly brute! I ought to be locked up!'

'So you ought,' she agreed coldly, and burst into tears.

There was a thoughtfully-placed bench by the gates of Lauderdale House, just right for a lovers' reconciliation. There they kissed and mutually apologised and vowed it should never happen again, never.

'But Albert, dear . . .'

'What, pet?'

'Do you *have* to drink?'

'Well, seein' as I'm not a camel –'

23

'No, don't joke. I mean, why do you go into those places? 'Tisn't as if you knew anybody in them; and I know you're not *always* thirsty, though you were just now and I ought to have made allowances. Oh, I know they say that about drowning your sorrows in drink, but you don't need to do that, do you?'

He studied her upturned pleading face.

'No, 'course not. Be a shame if I did. Dear, I don't know what it is, I've never thought. P'raps it's because I'm not allowed it at 'ome. You ought to hear my old man! "Ne'er a drap o' yon speerituous evil crosses ma threshold!" It doesn't, neither. Blimey, when they sing sacred songs of a Sunday evening Mother gets an encore for *Lips that touch Liquor shall never touch mine.* So you see it makes me feel free, like, to take a drink outside.'

She patted his cheek. 'Can I tell Mama? she worries a bit, you know, when you take me home and it's on your breath.'

'Of course. And I won't touch the stuff when we're married, cross me heart I won't.'

'Married! Oh, Albert, I can't hardly believe it. This time next year ...'

'Perhaps before that. If I take Watkins's work over when he goes I'll get an extra three bob a week. It'll mean staying later at nights, o' course ...'

'Oh, never mind that! I can get a bit of extra work too, Lady Evans said she'd be glad for me to go and give her Martha a hand with the sewing, any night I liked. Then we can put a bit by.'

Through the still evening air the bell of Highgate Chapel clock tolled nine. Albert pulled her to her feet.

'Come on, dear. Time we were getting back. I've properly spoiled the evening, 'aven't I, rotter that I am! Oh yes, I know it. And I tell you something, Marianne – I mean not to waste my money on drink after this. What's the odds, anyway? When we're married we'll 'ave a bottle of wine once a week, won't we.'

She stretched up to kiss him. 'Oh Albert, you're so good! And I'm sorry I was a bad, cross thing. Oh, I can just see

24

our little home, and the dinner-table, with those plates we saw with the ivy round.'

'A nice little barrel of oysters?' Albert suggested.

'Yes, and a duck with green peas –'

'Or a tasty bit of boiled mutton, or suet dumplings –'

'And to finish with, Spanish Cream with tipsy Jam!' Marianne clapped her hands and broke into a dancing step. 'Oh, look at the end of the sunset over there! Isn't it wonderful? Isn't *life* wonderful?'

Curiously enough, a bottle of wine was to change life for them.

CHAPTER THREE

It was quite an ordinary bottle of wine, a roughish Burgundy which would have cost one-and-threepence over the counter, but was priced at two shillings by the proprietors of Rosherville, anxious to recoup their lavish expenditure on the pleasures they provided for customers.

That Saturday had been one of those rare golden days that only come in September, when the stuffiness of August has gone and the air is heady, the roses in their third triumphant blooming. Marianne and Albert had not met for a week; he had worked late on the papers concerning a large estate which was being handled by his firm, copying documents until he felt that his eyes were standing out like chapel hatpegs, as he put it, while Marianne had obliged Lady Evans's Martha with her assistance. By a happy chance, her birthday fell on the Saturday.

She had made herself a new dress for the planned outing, of Pompadour sateen in a rich pink; a tiny frill of cotton lace framed her throat, a row of imitation pearl buttons fastened the blouse from neck to the high-belted waist. A cluster of rosebuds crowned her little shepherdess hat, her cheap cotton gloves were spotlessly white.

'You look a treat,' said her mother, stepping back to admire the effect. 'Here, you want a finisher-off just there, at the top. I've got just the thing.' She whisked something from behind her back and fastened it round Marianne's neck. 'There! that's better.'

'Whatever . . . oh!' Marianne stared at her image in the mirror. The little neck-frill was now encircled with a black ribbon, from which hung a silver locket, its centre a cluster of flowers painted on enamel.

'Oh! it's lovely! But Mama, it's not for me, is it? You gave me the gloves!'

'If a girl can't have two presents when she's eighteen,'

said Harriet, 'I don't know when she can have. Never look a gift-horse in the mouth, my dear, for it might bite you.'

At Fenchurch Street Station Albert was waiting, a flower in his button-hole and a small parcel in his hand. They kissed rapturously.

''Appy birthday, darling, 'appy birthday, and many of 'em! Lor, you look nice!' He closed her hands round the parcel. 'For a good girl.'

'Oh, Albert! Oh, what can it be? Am I to open it?'

'Soon as we're on the train you can. It mightn't be safe now.'

'Why? is it one of them Russian bombs?'

'That's right.' He held it to his ear. 'Ticking away lovely.'

Entwined, laughing, they boarded the train and occupied a double seat which exuded clouds of dust, motes dancing in the sunshine that filtered through the dirty carriage window. Other holiday-makers filled up the compartment, laughing and chattering, hushing children, eating sweets from paper bags.

'Now for it!' Marianne was carefully removing the wrappings, so painstakingly secured by loving but clumsy hands. Last of all came a handkerchief, protecting the precious centre. Marianne removed it.

'Albert! You *never* – oh!' She was speechless, holding in her hands like a saint's relic a small unglazed figurine. It represented a cupid, rosy and golden-haired, its sex hidden by a fortuitous wisp of blue drapery, small wings of the same blue springing from its shoulders, across which lay a milkmaid's yoke. From each end of this hung not a bucket but a heart, tastefully coloured the pink of sugared almonds. Fifty years from that day of 1880 a girl with a faint look of Marianne about her would push it contemptuously aside. 'That old Victorian rubbish!' she would say. 'Send it to the church sale.'

But here and now it was between her ancestress's hands, warm and worshipped.

27

'Albert, you shouldn't have. Oh, I don't know what to say.'

'Nothing *to* say. I remembered you looking at it in that shop window and saying it was what you'd buy first of all if we 'ad a mantelpiece to put it on. So I thought, well, let's grab it now and let the mantelpiece follow. And I went back and bought it.'

It had cost half a crown, a substantial slice out of Albert's few shillings. But today's jollifications could be paid for out of the extra money Mr. Simpson had given him for working long hours this week.

The sun was still high when they reached Gravesend, and crossed the river on the crowded ferry-boat. With the rest of the passengers, they made their way up to the Gardens' entrance, to the faint strains of the brass band which played at Rosherville Pier to welcome those who had travelled the slower way by steamboat. Past the turnstile, they were in the familiar paradise of trees and flowerbeds, fountains which were also fish-pools, and notices appealing to litter-fiends not to scatter refuse where it would interfere with the beauty of the scene. Other warnings indicated that while Every Flower was born to Fade, it would nevertheless cost you 2s. 6d. if you were caught picking one.

They strolled up to the tower above the chalk cliff, that looked towards the wide Thames, and beyond to Purfleet and the dockyards. On the river dignified sail mingled with fussy steam; a China clipper made her slow way up river, like a great swan. Green woods and valleys basked in the distance. Marianne sniffed luxuriously.

'Lovely, lovely air. I suppose it's from Kent. I'd like to go to Kent, Albert.'

'You're in it now, by rights. But we'll go to the country, proper, next year. Margate, p'raps.'

'Folkestone's nice, too.'

'Yes, Folkestone's nice.'

Back to the lawns for the ceremonial shrimp tea, the china cupid on the table between them, blandly smirking as Marianne tapped the hearts in turn so that they swung gently on their golden links. Tea over, they strolled round the museum, passing, as usual, by the kitten with two heads preserved for posterity in a jar of spirits ('Wonder whether they'd have fed 'em both at once, if it'd lived?' Albert speculated) and rested in the bijou theatre, to be entertained by a soulful lady who sang *Watching for Pa*, and a whiskered gentleman who requested musically to be Rock'd in the Cradle of the Deep, after which they joined voices in the duet *O that we Two were Maying*; and the lovers, with not the vaguest notion between them of what maying might be, smiled at each other and held hands.

Soon, before the sun was down, the torch-lamps began to come out among the trees, like giant fireflies, and the coloured lights surrounding the Baronial Hall to make a fairy garland of themselves, while inside the Hall musicians were beginning to tune up for the evening's dancing.

They danced together, the dashing Lancers and the languorous Waltz, and the jolly Quadrilles, until they were hot and happily thirsty. At Albert's suggestion, they subsided at one of the small tables, and ordered meat pies, the delicacy of the day, recommended by the waiter as 'Fit for 'er Majesty, Gawd bless 'er. Somethink to drink with 'em, sir?'

Albert studied the bill of fare. 'What about a bottle of wine, then, seeing it's an occasion? – Madam's birthday,' he added grandly for the waiter's enlightenment.

'Oh, in that case, sir, this is the very thing,' and before Marianne could object the bottle was between them, uncorked.

'Shipped by Dubois Freres,' read Albert, pronouncing the names as spelt. 'French. Just right, eh, love?'

'Well, I don't think . . . Albert, I don't really like wine. Couldn't I have something else?'

'What, and me drink the lot? Come on, be a sport,' and he filled her glass with the dark ruby fluid. She shuddered at the first mouthful, gulped down the second like medicine; and then, to her own surprise, began to enjoy the taste and held out her glass for more. The waiter, finding trade slack, sidled up to their table and indulged in some speculations

29

concerning the probable reaction of Her Majesty to the defeat of Lord Beaconsfield in the recent election, adding that it was Lord Beaconsfield himself, when merely Mr. Disraeli, who had put up some of the money to buy the land from Mr. Rosher, before it was ever a pleasure-garden. Finding them disappointingly indifferent to the information, he drifted away in search of more rewarding customers.

Marianne's cheeks were glowing and her eyes sparkling as the wine coursed through her. Her speech was a trifle slurred, which Albert, himself affected by the drink, found highly amusing. He reached across the table and laid his hand over hers; her eyes were laughing with a recklessness which had never been there before.

' 's very hot in here,' she said, 'less go f'r a walk.'

'Pleasure's mine.' He rose and bestowed the excessive tip of a penny for the waiter under a plate, then took Marianne's arm. Unsteadily, they wavered out into the Gardens, which were now mysterious with shadows and the stars of the gas-lamps, twinkling as leaves stirred by the night breeze moved to and fro across them. Here and there a classic statue gleamed palely against dark shrubs; a kilted woman with a bow and arrow, a crescent in her hair, a helmeted youth who seemed to be flying, small wings growing from his heels; an athlete hurling a discus. Marianne giggled; at another time she would have averted her eyes from male nudity, even in marble.

'Whatever's that he's wearing? Or does it grow on him?'

'It's a fig-leaf,' replied Albert, faintly embarrassed.

Marianne appeared to find this answer very funny. 'Fig-leaf! Fig-leaf!' she repeated, laughing unrestrainedly. 'Wonder how he keeps it on?' They strolled on, further and further away from the Baronial Hall and the coloured lights. Now and then another couple would come into view, strolling as they were, or sitting merged and still on one of the rustic benches framed in arbours of yew. Music floated to them through the trees, a Viennese waltz; a girl's laugh rang out. Some animal or bird in the zoo uttered a thin cry, and was answered. Marianne clung tighter to Albert.

'S'like being in a jungle,' she said. 'Ever so mysterious.'

They passed the last of the line of lighted statues, a woman's stalwart armless torso.

'That's Venus,' said Albert. 'I seen a picture somewhere...'

Venus. Marianne's confused mind struggled with a memory. The Black Venus: her great-grandmother's love-charm doll. Somehow, the thought of it was not repulsive any longer; it was even a bit exciting.

The path they were treading was almost invisible by now. They were closely entwined, arms round each other's waists, Albert's cheek pressed against her hair. The rosebud bonnet had been left behind, unnoticed, at the table. They were in a little enclosed glade, formed by a great oak-tree and ranks of bushes. Marianne leant back against the tree and held out her arms to Albert. She clasped him closer than ever before; he kissed her as he had never done in all their chaste courtship. Nature, not experience, taught him as he fumblingly unbuttoned her blouse and pushed down the chemise beneath it, so that he could hold the warm young breasts in his hands, and feel their excitement. He struggled with her belt, but she was already unbuckling it, and dragging at the hooks and eyes which fastened her skirt, until it fell at her feet. Panting with desire, Albert pressed himself against her, kissing her deeply, until without conscious thought they slipped to the ground, and she felt his weight above her, his head blotting out the branches and the stars.

So it was that from the magic of a September night, of wine and music, there came into being the spark of life that would be baptised Clemence, and, much later, would be renamed Sarah.

Harriet, hard-worked at Jay's as the gentlefolk streamed back to London from the country at the start of the winter season, was too tired by evening to be alert to the change in her daughter. Marianne was a bit quiet, of course, but that was natural, contemplating a big step like marriage as she was. She seemed to have less appetite than usual for

31

their early breakfast on the increasingly dark mornings of October, and once or twice surprised her mother by saying that she was too tired to go out on her weekly evening with Albert. When she did go, she sometimes came back depressed and anxious only to go to bed.

It was the end of November when Harriet entered the little bedroom in time to see Marianne standing by the down-tilted mirror, struggling with the fastenings of her skirt. As her mother watched, she turned and looked at the reflection of her waist in profile, sighing heavily. Harriet moved into the room and shut the door.

'Oh!' Marianne jumped. 'I didn't hear you come in.'

'You wouldn't. I've got me slippers on. What d'you expect me to wear about the house, boots and spurs? All right, Marianne; you needn't hide it any more. I've got eyes.'

Marianne sank on to the bed, tragic-faced. 'Oh, Mama, what am I going to do?'

'How long is it?'

'Going on three months.'

'I see,' said Harriet grimly. 'I've got a few words to say to Mr. Albert Moffat.'

'Oh no, don't, don't! Please don't say anything to him. It was my fault . . . I mean, I don't know whose fault it was. But don't speak to Albert.'

'I'll have to, sooner or later, won't I? We've got to fix the wedding. Not that it'll be the sort of wedding I wanted for you, but that's neither here nor there. It's the child we've got to think of.'

Tears were trickling down Marianne's cheeks. 'I don't want to think. Oh, leave me alone, please do.' Harriet joined her on the bed, and put an arm round her shaking shoulders. 'Come on,' she said, 'what is it? These things happen, you know. Tell your old Mama.'

But no amount of coaxing or questioning would extract any sense from Marianne, and in the end Harriet left her. Marianne crawled wearily on to the bed and covered herself with a blanket. She lay staring at the cracks in the ceiling, at the brown stain by the picture-rail where the rain came in, but the landlord wouldn't do anything about it: at a bad sepia engraving of *The Light of the World*, the thorn-crowned Christ knocking patiently at the door of mankind's heart. The words of a hymn drifted into her mind.

> 'O Jesu, thou art standing
>   Outside the fast-closed door,
> In lowly patience waiting
>   To pass the threshold o'er . . .'

How did it go on?

> 'O love that passeth knowledge,
>   So patiently to wait!
> O sin that hath no equal
>   So fast to bar the gate!'

She began to pray brokenly. 'O Jesus I'm sorry I haven't been to church more. I'm sorry I was so wicked at Rosherville. Oh, please forgive me, and make me a child of God and I'll be good, I will. Please tell me what to do, in Your name!' The painted eyes looked sadly back at her; behind the haloed head were waving branches against a night sky, stars shining through them, just as there had been that night . . . She turned her face into the pillow and wept.

On Sunday morning Marianne went to church, to St. Mary's in the High Street. Harriet, though not of a religious turn, offered to go with her, but Marianne refused. She would go alone and make her petition alone. In a back pew, her short cloak hugged round her, disguising what she felt everybody in the congregation must be staring at, she knelt and sat as the service proceeded, joined in the hymns, substituted her own prayers for those in the book. 'O God, make Albert love me again!'

For Albert, kind loving Albert, seemed to dislike the sight and touch of her now. She didn't know the instinctive male fear of being trapped and imprisoned by marriage. Albert had gone white with shock when she had told him she was pregnant. Then, to her horror, he had suggested a way out.

33

'There's women that – that could get rid of it for you.'

She looked at him unbelievingly. 'You don't mean that, Albert? You don't mean you'd let me . . .' She choked. There had been a girl at Madame Billings's who had got in the family way and whose boy had given her the money for a back-street abortion. Over their sewing the girls whispered.

'Florrie won't be coming back. I went to see her, and she was ill, sort of raving and talking nonsense. She didn't know me. There was blood all over the place. She said the old woman did it with a knitting needle . . .' Whisper, whisper, in case Madam heard them talking about poor Florrie who would never come back to the workroom, because she was dead.

'I couldn't do that, Albert. I'm surprised at you for even thinking of it. You're very unkind!' She began to cry again, and Albert impatiently snapped, 'Oh, dry up! Snivel, snivel, snivel, that's all I get from you these days. I can't marry you yet, I tell you.'

'But w-why not?'

'No money, that's why. Think I can keep three on seventeen bob a week?'

'But why can't you ask Mr. Simpson to give you the rise now? And you'll get it at Christmas anyway. Oh, I don't understand you.'

How could she understand the storm of fear and revulsion that raged in Albert's heart? He was just twenty-one, a man in years but a boy in immaturity, unready for the responsibility of fatherhood. The pretty girl he'd courted had turned into a pale woman with an increasingly swollen body, always crying, crying, until he could hit her. He hated himself more than her. Sometimes he thought of doing away with himself; a razor perhaps. But he knew he would never do it. The sight of blood turned him up. There was always laudanum, morphine, of course, that was the way women usually killed themselves. But how much did you take, and how did it make you feel? Coward, coward, he shouted inwardly at his cringing self.

Sometimes he contemplated running away. He would

leave the office one evening with a week's wages in his pocket, and walk and walk, across the river, to one of the theatres on the Surrey side, where he could get work. He knew he could act, remember lines, sing if they wanted him to. If they didn't, he could shift scenery; anything. He'd grow a moustache and change his name to something like Alberto Moffatino. And Marianne would be all right. With her looks, once she'd had the kid, plenty of chaps would leap at the chance of marrying her.

In St. Mary's, the Vicar was pronouncing the Blessing. '. . . The love of God, and the fellowship of the Holy Ghost, be with us all evermore. Amen.' The organist broke into the closing voluntary, the worthies of Islington, in their best Sunday clothes, began to file out of the church. Marianne stayed in her pew until they were all gone, so that she should not have to shake the Vicar's hand and hear his greeting. For her prayers had not been answered, she knew. Nobody had listened; she could make Nobody hear. Unless, perhaps, the Devil, for inside her head she seemed to hear a soft voice saying: 'Don't marry Albert. Don't. Bring up the child yourself, and I will look after you both.' Who could be saying that, except the Devil? She hurried from the church, her head down so that lingering churchgoers would not recognise her.

That afternoon, as her mother took her Sunday nap, she went to the drawer that held table-linen, and drew from it the small package wrapped in silk. She placed the doll on the table, propped against a vase. She knelt, her hands clasped, and raised her eyes to the doll's fixed stare.

'Oh Black Venus, Aida Weydo, goddess of love, make Albert love me again! Make him marry me!'

She concentrated fiercely as she had not been able to do in church. When her strength began to fail she rose again from her knees, bowed to the doll, wrapped it up reverently and replaced it in the drawer.

At the same moment Albert, lounging moodily in the sitting-room of his parents' house, alone because they had gone to an afternoon service at the Chapel, felt a sudden warmth that didn't come from the fire. It seemed to fill his breast and his brain. An image of Marianne rose before him, pleading, lovely, tempting, holding out to him a tiny child, that turned its face to him, and showed him the face of Marianne in miniature. He jumped up, slapping his forehead. 'I've been a fool!' he shouted to the empty room. 'I've been a bloody fool!'

Two weeks later, on a wet December day, Albert Moffat and Marianne Dumas were joined in matrimony at St. Mary's Church, Islington.

CHAPTER FOUR

It seemed to Clemence that she remembered everything that had ever happened to her since the day she was born, though Mum said that couldn't be so, and she was not to tell fibs. Clemence knew better. She remembered, for instance, when she couldn't even speak and Mum and Dad were trying to make her talk to them. Mum said she was to call them Mama and Papa, but Dad told her not to be such a snob, and that Mum and Dad were what everybody called their parents. And Mum looked sharp at Dad, and said, 'What about *you*, then?', and Dad looked sulky and said that was nothing to do with it.

When she was older, and could make sense of what people were saying when she was in bed in the next room, supposed to be asleep, she learnt the reason for this. Dad's parents had said they didn't want to see him any more after he'd married Mum. They hadn't gone to the wedding nor even to the christening of Clemence; and when Dad had gone round there to tell them that another baby, a little boy, had been born and then died, his father had shut the door in his face. There was something about 'the wages of sin', too. What could these possibly be, Clemence wondered? She knew what wages were, her Dad and other Dads got them and gave their wives some money out of them every Friday night; and then Dad would go out and come back smelling of something funny, and be very loving and kind to her and Mum; and after the lamp was out she would hear sounds from the big bed, rustlings and creakings and Mum's soft giggle. But what was sin?

She asked her Grannie, who lived with them and always sat with her when Mum and Dad went out, and Sue, the little maidservant from the Foundling Hospital, had time off. Grannie, who was so gentle (and so pretty, Clemence thought, in spite of her hair being all grey) only laughed, and said she'd find out some day, and if she didn't she was too good for this world.

Sometimes Mum and Dad took her out with them, and when she was able to walk, 'such a noticing little thing', the neighbours said. The place where they lived was called Clerkenwell, which was an interesting place. There was a nice green where children in perambulators were admired by the people who strolled about there on Sunday afternoons, and where older children played games like cricket. Clemence's dad used to take her there and they'd play ball, with the special lovely ball made exactly like an orange that her grannie had given her. Dad was never tired of throwing it back to her. He was so proud to be seen out with his little daughter and hear the complimentary remarks made about her. 'Reg'lar little beauty, ain't she!' 'Where'd you get those big eyes, love?' Sometimes people Dad knew would tease him because Clemence was so dark and he was so fair, and make puzzling remarks about Mum having been to Margate for the weekend.

Because Clemence was so bright and had such a good memory, people enjoyed teaching her words and hearing her say them back. She could say quite big words, like 'infirmary' and 'donkey-cart'. Dad used to teach her songs, too; he knew a lot of them, and sang them in a very funny way. He would sing one, over and over, and she would sit on his knee, copying his voice and expression. There was a rather bad day when he was teaching her a new one, and Mum came in and heard her singing it, just the last chorus.

'What did Mr. Gladstone
Say in 'eighty two?'
(*spoken*) 'I'm sure *I* don't know. What did 'e? *I* don't know either. But –
(*sung, fortissimo*)
'Eve said to Adam,
The naughty little madam,
Oh, Adam, 'ave a quick one, do!'

Mum crossed the room in half a tick and smacked

Clemence round the ears, making her howl. Then she said to Dad, 'I thought I told you not to teach that child filth!' Clemence didn't hear any more because she was pushed outside and the door shut.

She was allowed to sing other things, though, like the rhyme Dad taught her when they went out walking along the City Road, which the rhyme was about.

'Up and down the City Road,
In and out the Eagle,
That's the way the money goes – Pop! goes the weasel!'

When she was very small Clemence would take a paper bag with her to burst at the word Pop! It made a very striking effect.

Sometimes Dad and Mum and Clemence would go for a walk past Sadler's Wells Theatre, and talk about how they met each other there. Mum's face, which was sometimes a bit sad, was always smiling and pretty at these times, and Dad looked as if he were very fond of her. When Mum stayed at home they would continue the walk to a large building called The Angel; Clemence supposed it was because it had a picture of one painted on a board outside. Dad would go in here, leaving her outside with strict instructions not to stir one foot till he came out, or to speak to *anyone*. So, when ladies patted her brown curls, or gentlemen with sly expressions begged her to come round the corner with them, where she would find a most beautiful sweet-shop, she returned a cold stare which often sent them away muttering that the child must be an idiot.

Once a very severe lady with shiny spectacles came up to her and said, 'Little girl, do you know that you are on the very threshold of a Haunt of Vice and Iniquity? Let me take you to our Chapel, and one of our missioners will give you an improving tract.' Clemence had never heard of tracts, improving or otherwise, but didn't think she would like them much, so she told the lady, in a phrase she'd heard somewhere, to go away, and the lady went scarlet and looked as if she were going to burst, and then marched away very quickly. When Dad came out of the Angel Clemence told him about this. He said: 'What did you say to her, love?' and Clemence told him. For a moment Dad looked as though he were going to burst, too, but with laughter; and then he went serious and said she must never, never say that word again, especially in front of Mum, or she'd get the spanking of her life.

Mum had a heavy hand when she was cross. When she wasn't, and sat quietly doing the sewing she took in for ladies now that she couldn't go out to work, she would tell Clemence stories, about plays, and princesses, and about her own family, the dark lady Marie-Cessette who lived in a hot country thousands of miles away, and the great French story-writer who was Marie-Cessette's son and Mum's grandfather, and wrote about some French soldiers called The Three Musketeers.

'I'd like to read,' said Clemence. 'Will you teach me, Mum?'

Mum just smiled and said she wasn't really clever enough, but some day Clemence would go to school. Then she would sing little French songs for Clemence to learn: not at all the sort of things Dad taught her, but *Sur le Pont d'Avignon*, or *Cadet Rousselle*, which they would clap out in rhyme together.

> 'Cadet Rousselle a trois beaux chats,
> Qui n'attrapent jamais les rats.
> Ah, ah, ah c'est vraiment –
> Cadet Rousselle est bon enfant.'

Mum said she didn't know what all the words meant, because she'd only learnt them by ear from her father, as Clemence was learning.

There was one thing over which Mum wasn't ever cross and Dad was. Ever since she was a baby, Clemence had seen people who weren't in the room at all, Dad said when she was old enough to describe them. 'Fibs!' he said. 'I don't like fibs.' It was no use saying that the people *had* been there, though she knew they had. There was a dark young man

40

with long hair and a pretty waistcoat, who held a sort of long wooden box up against his face, and drew a stick to and fro over it, and music played. Then there was an old, old man, very sad-looking, in funny clothes, a very long coat with buttons all down it, and frills at the bottom of the sleeves. He would sit in a chair and gaze into the fire, with his thin legs crossed, and she could see that his trousers stopped at the knees, and there were big silver buckles on his shoes. Something told her that while the dark young man belonged somehow to her and Mum, the old man belonged to nobody but the house itself. When she told Mum about him, Mum said that he'd probably lived there a long time ago, when the big room downstairs in the Johnsons' part of the house had been a drawing-room. Perhaps this had been his bedroom, and a sad place for him.

Only once (and it was before Mum told her the story of her family) Clemence saw a lady who was all black, as black as the Minstrels Dad had taken her to see. But they had paint on their faces, he said, and this lady's skin wasn't at all like theirs. She had a beautiful face, really beautiful, and a sort of tall hat-thing made of silk and flowers all wound round each other. Her dress was stripey, gold and red and blue, and the skirt stood out stiffly, not like Mum's. There were gold rings in her ears. She was bending over Clemence's bed so that the earrings hung forward, and her hands were on the side-rail that stopped Clemence falling out of bed; Clemence could see that though they were as black as anything the palms were pink.

When she told Mum about the black lady, Mum said nothing, but her lips went very tight. She went away and came back with a little silver chain which had a cross hanging from it: Clemence knew the man on the cross was Jesus, because she'd seen him in church. Mum put the chain round her neck.

'Wear this at night, dear,' she said. 'Promise me you'll always wear it at night.'

'Why can't I wear it at day, Mum?'

41

'Because people would think we're Romans, and we're not.'

'What's a Roman?'

The conversation had been neatly turned.

When Clemence was five, in 1887, her mother's hourglass figure began to change. Clemence was delighted to know that she was going to have a little brother or sister, for she loved company, and her mother was strict about not letting her play in the street. 'You'll be going to school soon,' she was told.

'Why shall I?'

'Because the law says so. Everybody has to now when they're five.'

'Did you have to when you was a little girl?'

'No.'

'Why?'

'Because the law was different, that's why. Don't ask so many questions, child.' Marianne's hand went to her aching back, and she lowered herself carefully into a chair.

'Is it nice having babies, Mum?'

Marianne smiled wryly. 'Not very'.

'Is that why I'm to be sent down to Mrs. Johnson while you have it, so that I shan't cry?'

'That's right. Now run along and let Mum have a rest.'

It was dull at Mrs. Johnson's, though her rooms were the nicest in the house. The front one had a marble fireplace with faces on it which Clemence made up stories about. Mr. and Mrs. Johnson slept in an old four-poster with no canopy, only four legs sticking up in the air. Clemence thought it must be like sleeping in a table turned upside down. Mr. Johnson was a postman who got up so early that Mrs. Johnson was alone all day and welcomed Clemence's company and entertaining conversation. She would sit in the rocking-chair beside the marble fireplace, knitting for one of her apparently numberless grandchildren, pushing her spectacles down her nose the better to observe Clemence's dramatic entrances dressed up in clothes from the Johnson wardrobe. The most striking of her 'turns', Mrs. Johnson agreed, was that in which she appeared in Mr. Johnson's best overcoat, which completely enveloped her and trailed behind, his brown bowler hat resting on her ears, and some red stuff suspiciously like rouge dabbed in big circles on her round cheeks. 'Here we are again!' she would cry. 'Now is there anything what I can go for to bring, for to fetch, for to carry for you, Miss? Who am I, Mrs. Johnson, who am I?'

'Why, the clown in the pantomime, o'course, my dear.'

Another impersonation involved the discarding of Clemence's skirt and the audience's acceptance of Mr. Johnson's cane in the role of a rapier, together with its tolerance of longcloth knickers displayed in their entirety. As this apparition was seen to 'enter fighting' an invisible opponent, Mrs. Johnson was supposed to enquire in astonishment: 'Why, whoever can this be?' to which the performer would reply triumphantly, 'Oh, that's a mys-tery. Miss Terry, see?'

'There now! that *is* clever. I don't know where you get it all from, Clem, I don't, I'm sure,' resuming her knitting. 'Unless it's from your Dad, for he's *quite* a card. Your Mum, now, she's a quiet lady, but ever so nice.' Reminded of the situation of the quiet lady at that moment, she glanced upwards, and was thankful, not for the first time that day, that these old houses were so well-built, and you couldn't hear what was going on upstairs, not if a whole Regiment of Foot was to march across the floor in their boots and spurs; and just as well, for that poor thing didn't have babies easy, not according to what Mrs. Dumas said.

'When I had all mine,' she told Clemence with seeming irrelevance, 'there was straw down in the street and the knocker muffled with a glove round it.'"

'Why?'

'To keep the place quiet, that's why. It was always done when persons was very sick or lying-in. Nowadays there'd be no use in it, what with all this traffic about and horses continually mounting the pavements and running over people, like you're always reading in the paper, and then those nasty Fenians that they say Mr. Parnell was one of them, well, Mr. Johnson did hear at St. Martin's, that's his headquarters, my dear, that one had been arrested with a bomb in his pocket, right outside Charing Cross Station, as he was landing from Ireland.'

Clemence had not been listening to Mrs. Johnson's commentary on current affairs, but to her own thoughts and sensations. She looked up with a lightened face. 'I think Mum's better,' she said.

Ten minutes later Harriet Dumas, tears of relief streaming down her cheeks, was telling them that Marianne had a baby boy.

Her struggle back to recovery was slow after a long, agonizing labour. She was unable to feed baby Charlie, so a wet nurse was enlisted. Mrs. Pigge, whose name convulsed Clemence to the point of being smacked for rudeness, bore an extraordinary resemblance to her animal namesake, being large and billowing of figure, healthy pink of complexion, and of that auburn hair-shade which goes with very small blue eyes and a few pale lashes. She was a washerwoman, happy in her work because it allowed her to stay at home and supervise her four children, all seemingly about the same age, and all in a perpetual state of being about to fall into the boiling copper and be rescued at its very edge. Every morning Charlie was taken to her cottage for his first and second feeds of the day, allowing Marianne to get some rest; for the third he came home, and his night refreshment was cows' milk from a bottle, to which he put up the strongest resistance.

Not that anything about poor little Charlie could be said to be particularly strong. He was underweight at birth, pale and peevish, and seemed too oppressed by the long flannel robes which encased him to try to kick them off, as a healthy baby should do. In this tropic summer of Queen Victoria's Golden Jubilee, golden day following golden day throughout June, Charlie fretted, hot in his cumbrous clothes and the heavy blankets and covers which filled his second-hand basket perambulator, which had once held the stout form of Clemence.

He had trouble with his breathing. One night an angry doctor was fetched from bed because Charlie had turned purple and seemed to be choking, while Marianne agitatedly held him in every position which could possibly be supposed to help him.

'Convulsions, ordinary convulsions,' snapped the dishevelled doctor, and ordered that Charlie should be placed in a hot bath, which eased him considerably. On another night he began to emit a loud crowing cough, a terrifying animal sound, his face blue and his tiny hands clenched. His mother panicked. 'Albert, he's dying, baby's dying! Get the doctor, quick! Oh, hurry, do!'

Gaping with huge yawns, Albert dragged on long pants, trousers and shirt, fastened his boots anyhow over unsocked feet and threw his greatcoat over his shoulders. Good thing it was a hot night, he thought, reeling with only half-banished sleep as he made his way to Dr. Lumley's house half a mile away. After five minutes of patient knocking the doctor himself answered, nightcapped and scarlet-faced with fury. To Albert's stammered explanation he returned a brusque answer. 'Now listen, Moffat, I've been called out once this week in the middle of the night to that child of yours. I told your wife what to do, and if she can't deal with common infant ailments she'd better get a nurse in. I've been up till midnight with a difficult confinement and I'll thank you to go back and tell your good woman that a doctor's time is valuable. Good night to you.'

'But it isn't – but it's different . . .' poor Albert began, only to have the door slammed in his face He arrived home prepared for the worst, to find Marianne gazing incredulously on while her daughter handled the situation with skill and aplomb. Roused by the noise, Clemence had arrived on the scene fully awake, in the way of healthy childhood. She took Charlie from his weeping, rocking mother. 'It's all right, Mum, don't take on. It's only croup. Betsy's little sister had it and she made the same noise.' Betsy was a child down the street with whom Clemence had been

45

strictly forbidden to play; but this was not the moment to remind her of it.

'What must we do, then?' Marianne asked meekly.

'Betsy's Mum got a hot cloth and put it round baby's throat and then made her sick. You get the cloth and I'll fetch the ipecac.' Professionally she propped the whooping Charlie up against the pillows, and brought from the shelf the bottle of ipecacuanha wine, that loathsome emetic so dreaded of the Victorian child. The hot cloth was applied, and Marianne held Charlie while a teaspoonful of the stuff was forced down his throat. 'It always works,' Clemence said complacently; and it did. Charlie, now quiet and breathing normally, was changed and cleaned up, and the dirty linen rolled up by Clemence and put out of sight. 'I'll take it to Mrs. Pigge in the morning, Mum, and Charlie can sleep in my bed tonight.'

There was nothing for Marianne and Albert to do but return to their own bed, thankful and wondering.

'She's a marvel, that little 'un,' said Albert. 'I reckon there isn't another kid could have done that. And not six yet . . .'

Marianne moved against his shoulder. 'She's a woman, not a kid, Albert. She's going to be a wonderful mother one day. I wish I was like her.'

Albert put his arms round her. 'You're a beauty, old girl. Give us a kiss.' He felt her turn her head towards Clemence's bed. 'It's all right, she's off already.' His hand cupped her breast. For a moment she resisted. 'It's too soon – after Charlie . . .'

But her body was responding to him; there was no going back.

After that night Charlie improved. At Mrs. Pigge's suggestion that in view of the hot weather he might do better with only a light cotton coverlet over him in his perambulator, 'being as my Beaty, what you might call 'is foster-sister, came out terrible in blotches till our Tommy takes 'er out in 'er birthday suit and they clears up like a miracle.' Beaty's perambulator was only a wooden box on wheels, which also served her as a cot and was frequently shared by the family cat, to the horror of the neighbours, cats being generally considered Death to Babies. But Beaty thrived, crowed and gurgled, naked as a cherub but for a diaper, and Charlie, allowed like her to kick in the sunshine of the back-yard, grew plumper and more contented.

So by Jubilee Day itself, June 17, the Moffat family was able to take part in the general rejoicings at the celebration of their Queen's fiftieth year on the throne. It was a general holiday. Clemence, who had spent most of her young life in Clerkenwell and Islington, would always remember that glorious day as her introduction to London, a great, wonderful place quite different from the small streets she had known. They had piled into a blue omnibus at the Duke of York, Islington, hustled there by Marianne in time to get seats. Charlie had been left behind with Grannie for fear of his being damaged or over-excited. Clemence, twisted round on her seat with her nose pressed against the window, saw the great stations pass, King's Cross, the stately Midland Hotel, St. Pancras, Euston and its lovely classic arch, more like the approach to a mansion than a railway station. Along the Euston Road they jogged, other omnibuses and private vehicles jostling them, westward bound, as were the walkers crowding the pavements.

When they left the omnibus at Piccadilly, Clemence lost sight of London; all around her were people, pushing and shoving, shouting and laughing, all bigger than her and very frightening. Her father felt the desperate tug at his hand, and looked down at the unusual sight of his little daughter's blue eyes brimming with tears.

'Up we go, then!' he said, and hoisted her up, carrying her easily in one arm while his wife clung to the other. The crowd, laughing and good-natured, made a passage for anyone with a small child to carry, so that the Moffats soon reached a spot from which they could see the procession route. It was a splendid wide road, with a square at one end where pigeons fluttered about a column so high that it seemed to Clemence to pierce the sky. The four huge stone lions that guarded its base were almost invisible for the sightseers who crammed their backs and even perched on their manes and ears. People, people everywhere, craning forward against the restraining police guards, gathered on roofs, leaning from windows of bunting-decked buildings, chattering, speculating. A man carrying a banner inscribed WHAT ABOUT THE UNEMPLOYED was set on, the banner torn from him. Nearby a girl fainted in the growing heat, and was passed above the heads of the crowd to an ambulance. Marianne shrank against Albert as a man pushed past her waving a bottle and singing raucously, displacing her best white straw hat and crushing her bustle. It seemed that the waiting grew more and more unbearable; Clemence began to think seriously about crying.

And then, like a signal, the voice of Big Ben boomed twelve. From the Mall a far-off crowd roar swelled and swelled, generating a wave of electric excitement among those who waited in Whitehall. Then there was the blare of music, triumphal trumpets and drums, and the clatter of hooves, and the first horsemen came in sight. Clemence thought she would die with excitement at the sight of them, splendid dark-faced men wearing brilliant turbans, the Queen's escort of Indian cavalry. The crowd noise unified in a great roar of joy and welcome, of cheers and shrieks and handclapping, as, with high-stepping dignified trot, six spanking cream horses came into view, harnessed together in pairs, gorgeously caparisoned in leather and brass, drawing a large open landau. Two ladies in waiting sat demurely, backs to the horses, facing a small figure in black. Instead of the jewelled crown Clemence and several thousand other people had been expecting, the Queen's neat grey head was topped with a black bonnet, its heart-shaped front edged with diamonds flashing back colours to the sun, above them a foam of white lace flowers. It was held in place by a white lace scarf whose ends lay across her capacious bosom and the blue Ribbon of the Garter. She was unsmiling, she was sixty-eight years old, unrecognisable as the pretty blonde girl who had travelled the same route to her crowning fifty

48

years before. Yet somehow she looked magnificent, and Clemence, who would see other queens in another century, never forgot that plain, fat old lady, bowing stiffly to her subjects.

'God save the Queen! God bless you!' they yelled and shouted, and Clemence, bobbing up and down on her father's shoulder, shrieked 'The Queen! The Queen!' at the top of her voice. Tall Albert had propelled them into the front row: the landau was exactly opposite them now, Her Majesty bowing in their direction; and Clemence would always swear that it was for *her* alone, little Miss Moffat, that the down-turned royal mouth lifted and broke into an amazingly jolly toothy smile. The crowd became hysterical at the sight of it, and amid the tumultuous waving of hats and Union Jacks the landau moved away down Whitehall, the royal princes who followed it in all the glory of full dress uniform seeming an anti-climax. But how splendid they were! How splendid it all was, that golden day of the Golden Jubilee, for all that Mum got hot and tired and Dad rather merry on bottled beer, and Clemence herself had nothing like enough to eat, in spite of a surfeit of so-called Jubilee Winkles. When, much too late, she went to bed, her tight-shut eyes could see nothing but the Queen's smile and the diamonds and lace on her bonnet. It would be nice to be Queen, she thought, seeing herself bowing from side to side to yelling crowds. Only, of course, she would be very beautiful, and on the whole she thought she wouldn't wear a bonnet, but a beautiful glittering crown.

At home, bedtime was put off because Dad had guessed rightly that from the attic window one could see the display of Brock's fireworks at the Crystal Palace, seven miles away. Standing on a chair, rapt with wonder, Clemence gasped as the 'Niagara of Fire' streamed through the air, an explosion of diamonds; and sparkling cascades of green and crimson and gold leapt up like rejoicing stars. 'Oooh! it's like Heaven!' she cried. 'If only there was Angels.'

It was a wonderful month, that unforgettable June. London was still gay with decorations, a spirit of happiness in the air, the weather unblinkingly perfect. When Dad was at work, Marianne and Clemence would go by buses or trams to 'the country', which for them was Kew and its flowers and trees, or high Hampstead, where you could sail a toy boat on the ponds or fly a kite (Clemence had no kite, but loved to see those of other children taking wing); or even, for a penny, ride a fat patient donkey. Marianne was slender again; the pretty young woman and the plump amiable child drew many eyes. At weekends Dad was with them, a dashing figure in his cheap but cheerful striped blazer and white straw hat. He took them to Lord's and the Oval, where white-clad figures ran about doing things inexplicable to Clemence, and Dad shouted approval and instructions to gentlemen called Hornby, Read, Abel, and others. Clemence found it all very boring and went to sleep, waking with a start as the teams strolled back to the pavilion, umpires drew stumps, and swallows darted over the deserted pitch, in pursuit of evening-flying insects.

On the first Friday of July came an end to the idyll. It was half-past six. Clemence was bored with her doll, Millie-Mollie, which Grandma had made for her, an ingeniously designed creature with a head at both ends and different skirts. Standing on the horse-hair sofa Clemence propped her chin on her hands and surveyed the street through the built-out bow window filled with pots of geranium. Suddenly she called out 'Mum, Dad's home!'

Marianne was in the kitchen. 'What, already? It's nothing like his time.' Wiping her floury hands on her apron, she opened the door for her husband. 'You're early, dear.' After their kiss she sniffed. 'Brandy?'

'Only one. Well, two. All on my ownio. That's a good smell. What's for supper?'

'Steak-and-kidney. Some don't deserve it, drinking.'

But the pie was delicious, Mum good-humoured, Dad cheerful but with an unusually pensive air on him. As though he were thinking about something quite different, thought Clemence, accepting a choice titbit from his fork.

The meal over, Albert sat back in his chair. At this point

they usually moved away from the table to comfortable chairs. Clemence felt a strange silence fall, as though things were happening which both of her parents knew about. They were looking at each other, Dad smiling in a not real way, Mum intensely serious.

'Marianne,' he said, 'I've left Simpson.'

His wife's hand flew to her mouth. 'You've – what?'

'I've left. I'm not going back. I've been there ten years and more. I'll be there all me life if I don't watch out. It's getting me nowhere.'

Marianne's face was white. 'What are we going to do?'

Outside a barrel-organ was playing *Love's Old Sweet Song*. In the tension of the room it seemed that the tune repeated itself several times before Albert spoke. In fact, only a few more notes had sounded.

'I don't know what you're looking like that for,' he snapped. 'I'm going into the theatre.'

'The *theatre*?'

Albert was heavily sarcastic. 'I s'pose you *'ave* 'eard of the theatre? I seem to remember your being a devotee of it some time back.'

'Yes, but . . . you mean you're going to act?'

'Ho, no. I shall perform poses plasteeks in the foyer, clad in a mere wisp of butter-muslin, to attract the Fair and Frail. Seats all prices.'

'Don't be stupid!' Marianne flared. 'Are you going to be an actor aren't you? Can't you talk sensible English for once?'

'All right, then,' he said, sulky. 'I've been engaged as walking gentleman at the Olympic.'

'How much?'

'It's not bad for a start –'

'*How much?*'

'Eighteen bob a week.'

'Eighteen?' His wife's voice rose to a shriek. 'Half of what you're getting now and no prospects, just to show yourself off on the stage, that you're not trained for and ought to have got over long ago, and how are we going to manage?

51

There's Mrs. Pigge to pay and Sue's wages, and clothes for Clemence to go to school, and – oh, you're mad, you're mad!'

The door opened, and Harriet's pretty, weary face appeared round it. 'Whatever are you two shouting about? They can hear you in the street.'

Marianne turned a tragic face to her mother. 'Albert's left his job. He's going to be an actor. So we'd better make up our minds to starve, hadn't we?'

'Starve!' Albert shouted. 'What are you going on about? I'll see you don't starve, won't I? Think I'm a fool? Oh, Gawd, she's off.' Marianne had burst into wild tears, her face buried on her arms across the table. Her mother gently touched her shoulder, and was shaken off. Clemence had often seen Mum cry, but never like this. Her own throat swelled and she felt her eyes stinging in sympathy. At last Marianne raised her flushed, tear-drenched face. 'There's one thing none of you knows,' she said. 'I'm expecting again.'

CHAPTER FIVE

Whether it was the unaccustomed sunshine or the Spirit of Jubilee that had caused Albert to give notice to the firm he had worked for since boyhood, he neither knew nor cared. He only knew that he was in the second half of his twenties, and that unless he took swift action he would spend the rest of his life working perched on a high stool scribbling or adding up, the slave of the Law. Was he not born for better things? Frequent glances into the dark fly-spotted mirror hanging outside his office assured him that the cares of fatherhood had not aged him; nor had Time decreased his resemblance to the ladies' idol, Mr. William Terriss. It was time he escaped.

Excusing himself from the office for an hour, 'to have a tooth pulled', he made his way along Holborn to Drury Lane, pausing when he got there to buy himself a fortifying glass of brandy and water, at the Queen of Bohemia, where the lovely, legendary Winter Queen, daughter of James I, had lived out the end of her days, before old Craven House forgot its aristocratic days and became a pub, and a low one at that. The Lane was a narrow street of old, doddering houses, Tudor gables leaning across it as though in conversation, dark and unsavoury alleys, richly carved doorways leading to the establishments of old-clothes dealers. Next to the pub, on the ground that had also held part of Craven House, was the Olympic Theatre.

It was a small playhouse with a long history of sensational productions and starry names. Albert had read an advertisement stating that it was to reopen under Entirely New Management in a season of melodrama. A curious time to reopen, when so many of the richer playgoers would be going out of town, and those who stayed were thinking of outdoor pleasures. But the Olympic had had a curious career. It was just the kind of place to take an inexperienced

53

enthusiast, Albert thought. So here he was, to keep an appointment with one A. Hewitt, manager.

The stage-door keeper, in his gloomy little box, looked as though he, like the entrance lobby, could do with a good dusting and polishing. To Albert's enquiry for the manager's office he returned no answer, but jerked a thumb in the direction of a pair of double doors studded with notices, which appeared to have been there a long time. Albert went through the doors and fell heavily down a step on the other side, landing painfully on one hand. The shock did nothing to bolster his confidence, but he batted the dust of the floor from his clothes as well as he could, and groped his way along the dim corridor. At the door marked MANAGER he stopped, gulped, took a deep breath and knocked. A light voice invited him to come in.

Behind a paper-cluttered desk, so big that it took up most of the small, shabby office, sat a young woman. Her blonde hair was piled up in crisp curls above a pink-and-white face which owed nothing to cosmetics; her figure in the tight-fitting tailored riding-jacket style, was round in the bosom and slender in the waist. She bestowed a bright enquiring smile on Albert. 'Yes?' she said.

'I – er – I was looking for the manager . . .' he began.

'I *am* the manager. Take a chair.'

Albert sat down with the suddenness of astonishment. 'The letter said A. Hewitt . . .'

'Quite correct. My name is Agnes Hewitt. This theatre has a tradition of female managers, as, of course, you know. The first was Madame Eliza Vestris.' Her manner was that of a pleasant but pedantic young governess; Albert was over-awed by it. She picked up a letter he recognised as his. 'You must be Mr. Albert Moffat.'

'That's right. I –'

'Now tell me all about yourself. Why do you wish to join my company?'

Albert told her. She listened carefully, taking notes, he thought (she was, in fact, sketching costume designs on her

54

blotting-paper), her head thoughtfully tilted. When he paused, she said:

'So you are entirely inexperienced, yet you have the audacity to apply for a professional engagement.'

'Well, I don't suppose –' said poor Albert, reaching for his hat.

'Sit down. I like audacity. You have courage and character, evidently, Mr. Moffat. You have also a good appearance, as I expect you have been told before.' She smiled at his flush. 'You are quite right to have confidence in your own ability; actors are not made out of sheep. But I'm sorry to hear you're married, with a growing family. Do you remember what the great Siddons said to Macready? "Study, study, study, my boy, and do not marry until you are thirty!" How do you propose to support your family on the very low salary which is all I could pay you?'

'I thought – if we did without our servant-girl – and our eldest, that's Clemence, stayed at home to help the wife instead of going to school yet . . .'

'You know that school attendance is compulsory from the age of five?' enquired Miss Hewitt. Albert did. 'But we've not been troubled so far,' he assured her. 'The Board inspectors don't get round our way much. People don't like 'em.'

'Even so, you think it fair to withhold education from your child.'

Albert had not so far given it any thought at all. 'She's very bright – she'll learn quick,' he said. Miss Hewitt tapped the desk briskly with a pencil. 'That brings me to a most important point: your voice.'

'My *voice*?'

'Your voice. Because we can never hear ourselves as others hear us, you are doubtless not aware that although the timbre of it is pleasant, you utterance is flat and your Cockney accent quite dreadful. Your grammar I will not mention, as it hardly affects a person who proposes to live by speaking other people's words. What I am saying to you, Mr. Moffat (for I see you find my remarks difficult to follow)

55

is that the only condition on which I will engage you is that for the coming season you will be satisfied with non-speaking parts only: you will, in fact, be a Walking Gentleman.'

'I see,' said Albert, unable to keep the disappointment out of his voice.

'You will also,' went on the alarming lady, 'take daily lessons in elocution. In the speaking of English,' she elaborated kindly, 'it will be very hard to eradicate your accent entirely, but we can try.'

'But – but – I can't afford lessons! And where would I go for them?'

Miss Hewitt looked surprised. 'I propose to teach you myself, of course. I am, as you have probably gathered, an actress, but I have always imagined the great pleasure of being a teacher. My life is a busy one' – she looked at the little fob watch pinned to her bosom by a bow of gold. 'I see I have already overrun the time I had set by for our interview. Very well. If you give notice to your employers today you will be free to report to me here at nine o'clock in the morning, a week on Monday. Your beginning salary will be eighteen shillings a week.' She gave him a brilliant smile and extended a beautifully-manicured hand. 'Good day, Mr. Moffat.'

As he was half-way through the door she beckoned him back.

'Just one thing more. No alcohol.'

Albert's face was a study in startlement. His concept of the theatre as a world of conviviality was shattered. He'd decided in the Queen of Bohemia that he was going to enjoy many jolly parties there with fellow-actors.

'Any person discovered entering my theatre with alcohol on their breath,' this dreadful woman was saying, 'will be instantly dismissed. I intend my little theatre in Wych Street to be beyond reproach. Thank you.'

'And thank *you*,' Albert muttered; but only when he was safely out in the corridor.

Clemence decided that on the whole the day her father entered the theatre was the best day of her life so far. Certainly, Mum was snappy, depressed because she was losing her figure again and wouldn't be able to wear her new swan skirt; and Charlie was teething painfully, no easy baby to look after even though she loved him so much. And money was scarce, of course. But her father was a different person, happy in his work, more confident in bearing; he was even beginning to sound different, like a proper gentleman, after a few weeks of Miss Hewitt and those dreary, endless repetitions of '*H*acking, *h*acking, *h*acking on the *h*ard *h*igh road' (if we have aspirations we must have aspirates, Mr. Moffat) and the painful stumbling through the most fiendish trap for actors ever penned by Shakespeare, Prospero's invocation, 'Ye elves of hills, brooks, standing lakes, and groves.' When Albert was half-way through it he always began to sweat at the mess he knew he was going to make of the rest.

He could generally manage 'heavenly music', but had the greatest difficulty with 'this airy charm': it had the most infuriating way of turning into 'hairy'. Still, he was making progress.

It was Miss Hewitt, essentially kind-hearted, who transformed Clemence's life like a Pantomime Good Fairy. She was not by any means unaware of Albert as a man, and it did not escape her eye that he was obviously not eating very well since he joined her company. One day she said to him at the end of a lesson:

'You're finding your salary inadequate, are you, Mr. Moffat?'

Albert shamefacedly admitted it. Little Sue had been sent back to the Foundling Hospital, who fortunately had another place for her, and Clemence was wonderful as a mother's help, but ... well, money will only go so far.

Miss Hewitt sketched a feather boa flanked by a pair of gloves and a reticule. 'Your little daughter,' she said. 'You say she takes after you in vivacity – in a fondness for acting and reciting. Is she presentable – attractive?'

'Why, yes, indeed, Miss Hewitt. She's a proper card – I

mean a born actress. And pretty: big blue eyes and a lovely little round face.'

'Do you think, as this child is being deprived of education and the society of children of her own age, and spends her days looking after her little brother (which is noble work but can hardly be amusing) – do you think she would like to come to the theatre with you one or two evenings a week, and perhaps earn herself a little money? Would that please her?'

Albert stammered that it would, and that she was very kind, and Clemence would be up in the air about it. He was told to present her next day. 'But mind,' said Miss Hewitt, 'I shall only engage her if I find her suitable, so don't raise her hopes too high.'

That was how Clemence came to be in the most magic place she'd ever seen, not the front of the theatre, but the back, mysterious, dark and thrilling, with a smell about it which affected her as the scent of battle is said to affect war-horses. What was it? She sniffed luxuriously, standing in the corridor with her father, waiting for the door that said MANAGER to open. One day she would know that the smell was compounded of carpentry, glue, sweat, scent, dress-baskets and an indefinable ingredient.

The spell of it was upon Clemence already.

The door opened; a gentleman with a striking face and long hair came out, looking cross, and a voice called them in.

Clemence's first impression of Miss Hewitt was of a lady of radiant beauty, even more beautiful than the ladies in the Jubilee procession. She was not overawed, but studied this vision with interest, her head on one side like an inquisitive robin. Miss Hewitt returned her gaze, taking in with an audition-sharpened eye the sturdy figure, lively expression, the humour of the full childish mouth, the rosy face and rich brown hair, more the looks of a country child than of a London sparrow.

'How old are you, Clemence?' she asked kindly.

'Six, miss. But I'm big for me age.'

'Yes. I doubt that you'll grow to more than – let me see –

58

five feet four or thereabouts. Never mind, that's an excellent height. A woman should not be too tall. Oh,' she added casually, 'and you do know, Clemence, that we don't say "me age" but "*my* age." You know that, don't you?"

Clemence thought. 'Yes, miss.'

'Do you think you could soon learn to speak properly, by listening to me, and other ladies here?'

'Shouldn't be surprised, miss.'

'Good. Walk across the floor; go and fetch me that book from the chair. Thank you. She moves well, Mr. Moffat. Do you know that you have a comedy nose, child?'

Clemence wondered if this was something bad, but to be on the safe side shook her head.

'Yes, all great comediennes have that nose, just tip-tilted but not in the least turned-up. Miss Kate and Miss Ellen Terry both have it. Your father tells me you can sing. Will you sing for me now?'

Clemence pondered, then stood straight with her feet together and her hands clasped in front of her chest, as she had seen singers stand on the stage. Very confidently and clearly she sang, in a French accent as pure as her English accent was not.

> 'Au jardin de mon père,
> Les lilas sont fleuris . . .
> La caille, la tourtourelle,
> Et le joli perdrix;
> Auprés de ma blonde,
> Qu'il fait bon, fait bon, fait bon,
> Auprés de ma blonde,
> Qu'il fait bon dormir.'

Miss Hewitt's lips twitched, but she asked composedly, 'Do you know what that song means, Clemence?'

'No, miss. Mum learned it me.'

'"*Taught* it me"'!'

'Yes, miss. Taught it me.'

'Very good. You have a quick ear.' She turned to Albert. 'Your daughter will do very well, I think. Please bring her with you two or three times a week; not more, for she must not be kept up late too often. Tell your wife that she must have extra sleep in the mornings, to compensate. She may walk on in the present piece and learn something about stage movement. You would like that, would you, Clemence?'

The child's eyes were blue stars. 'Oh, *yes*, miss!'

'I am Miss Hewitt, Clemence, not "miss".'

'Yes, Miss Hewitt.'

A fearful doubt had struck Albert. 'Suppose the Board School people hear about it? Won't they come to make her go to school?'

'I will handle them, if they try,' replied Miss Hewitt calmly. 'Very well, Clemence. Your salary will be three shillings a week.'

For once in her life, Clemence was speechless. She flushed scarlet, and tears started to her eyes. At Miss Hewitt's kindly nod Albert led his daughter to the door. Outside, in the corridor, Miss Hewitt could hear the child's ecstatic cry. 'Dad, I'm an *actress*, with real money! Three whole shillings!'

Agnes Hewitt mused. Such a fine child, stalwart and handsome, quick-brained, with a quality which one professional cannot mistake in another. And yet – that pleasant but weak father, the claims of the other children, the temptations of the stage; what would become of Clemence, she wondered?

§   §   §   §   §

Clemence took to the stage like the proverbial duck to the pond. She loved her red dress and grey cloak, procured for her from the theatre wardrobe. She loved the noisy, demanding, orange-sucking, nut-chewing audience, roaring, booing, breathing an immense sigh of compassion at the maltreatment of stage innocents. She loved the company; Mr. Willard, the dark man she had seen that first day, who played leading roles, and pretty Miss Maud Milton, the heroine, and the funny man who played a policeman, and quiet little Miss Danvers who played her mother in the big scene and led her on by the hand.

And she adored the play. Called *The Pointsman*, it was a rip-roaring melodrama in which Mr. Willard was the smooth, accomplished villain, ready to inflict an unpleasant death on all the other characters, if required, in the character of a riverside tavern proprietor (which he didn't look like in the least, thought Clemence, who had seen a few tavern proprietors in her time, while in her father's company). The great moment of the play came with a wonderfully ingenious transformation scene, a signal-box being transformed into a stretch of railway-line littered with corpses and horribly gory with red paint. After that there was a lot of shooting, and smoke, and coughing from the front rows of the stalls, until Mr. Willard received his final congé from another gentleman while in the act of shooting him, after menacing him in vain with a knife. How they shrieked and hissed him, out there in the pit and gallery! How he writhed on the boards, muttering 'Foiled! Foiled!' and when the curtain fell calmly got up and walked off, returning to tumultuous applause.

She learnt so much, that autumn; how one must never upstage another actor, speak with one's back to the audience, allow oneself to giggle, however unrehearsed the joke. She learnt that actors are the most delightful of the human kind, giving to others all the treasures of their charm and wit and beauty, if any, whereas ordinary people just talked. She learnt that the most modest of performers tended to address one, even in the green room, in tones which would easily have reached the back of the gallery; and to cap any anecdote told by somebody else with a very much longer, and funnier or sadder, as the case might be, anecdote about himself. She learnt that jealousy, even of her, a child, was always ready to flash its green eyes and stretch out a claw.

She didn't know that she was learning these things. They sank into her pliant, ready mind, imperceptibly, to emerge many years later.

There was nobody in the company anywhere near her age, except the stage carpenter's son, a stout and silent boy called Percy, who didn't seem very promising material for friendship. But Clemence had a friend, dear and constant. They met when she went timidly to the manager's office to collect her first week's wages. As she was handed her little envelope, with a maternal smile from Miss Hewitt, a golden-brown form uncoiled itself from where it had been lying beside the manager's desk. Slowly it advanced to inspect Clemence with interested sniffs. She hardly dared to breathe as the cold black nose delicately touched her knee, and the brown eyes were raised to her face with a gaze of human intelligence.

'You may stroke her,' said Miss Hewitt. 'She is very gentle.'

Tentatively Clemence's hand touched the silky head, caressed the long swinging ears. The graceful tail wagged, if such a dignified movement could be called wagging, in acknowledgment.

'Oh!' cried Clemence, enchanted, 'what a lovely dog, miss – Miss Hewitt! What sort is it?'

'A spaniel. Her name is Sheba.'

'Sheba,' Clemence breathed. 'Sheba.' The spaniel and the child looked into each other's eyes, and were friends.

.   .   .   .   .

At Christmas *The Pointsman* was taken off and the pantomime put on. It was a delirious experience for Clemence to be an actual part of that miraculous entertainment, a fairy in a gauze skirt of powder-blue, with gold tissue wings pinned to her pink bodice and a wand of gold tinsel. Miss Hewitt graciously assumed the role of Fairy Queen, Mr. Willard that of the Demon King, fiendish in a green spotlight. Albert was first a peasant dancing on the village green, an attendant on the Prince (Miss Milton in yellow satin tights) with a hunting-horn to show what he was meant to be, and finally a gorgeously dressed courtier when they all came down for the tableau that ended the evening. Clemence's mother and grandmother had been given seats, from which they could admire their Fairy, conspicuously bouncing among the paler and slimmer children hired for the occasion.

It was Marianne's last outing for some time. After Christmas the terrible yellow fogs descended like a death-pall on London, smoke from thousands of chimneys swirling down to form a miasma which blotted out all familiar landmarks. Cabs venturous enough to ply for hire became looming black shapes with carriage-lamps for staring eyes, horrible enough to be conveyances of the Demon King. Pedestrians clung to railings and crashed into pillar boxes; old people choked and coughed themselves into the graveyard.

But life and the play had to go on. At night Albert made his groping way through streets and squares to the Olympic, Clemence clinging to his hand. Her thin boots were poor protection against the cold slush which lay like a sodden carpet over pavements and cobbles, her coat, which was her only one, was threadbare. Even for a stalwart like Clemence the journey was hard going, Marianne protested.

'It isn't right for that child to tramp all that way, Albert. Goodness knows what she might catch, even supposing you aren't both run over one night.'

'Oh, Mum!' Clemence had learnt something about delivering dramatic appeals. Her face a study in piteous distress, she clasped her mother's skirt just as she had done in *The Pointsman*. 'I can't stop going! And it's three shillings a week. *Three whole shillings!* I'm very strong, really I am. Oh, Mum, please!'

Marianne gave in, of course. She was at the bovine stage of pregnancy when nothing mattered much except the growing, kicking life within her. So Clemence continued to go to the theatre when required, and even when not required, a blind eye being turned by the management on her evenings spent helping in Wardrobe with the mending and ironing of costumes, of drinking cocoa with Fred, the stage carpenter, while listening wide-eyed to his memories of Life and the Stage, and the great actress-manager Eliza Vestris, whom he'd adored. But the day came when little Charlie was taken ill, coughing, purple-faced. For hours they applied hot

63

cloths to his throat and chest, held bowls of steaming water under his nose, without effect. Clemence was sent out to a chemist for a mustard plaster and some Friar's Balsam, infallible remedies in his grandmother's opinion. By evening he was a little better; but it was to Clemence he turned for comfort. His hot, sticky small hand in hers, she sat by his bed and sang to him, her little French songs, ditties from the pantomime, ballads of astonishing range and variety remembered from the singing of Fred. From *Just a song at Twilight* she wandered into:

'Her eyes were as black as the pips of a pear,
   Her cheeks they were rosy – in ringlets hung her hair,
And her name was Isabella, with a gingham umbrella,
   And her father keeps a barber's shop in Is-ling-ton.'

That reminded her of the popular ballad which had actually started its life at the Olympic, and would be sung long after the theatre itself was only a few fragments of foundation-bricks beneath the sweeping curve of Aldwych.

'Long years ago in Vestminster,
   There lived a Ratcatcher's daughter,
Vell, she didn't qvite live in Vestminster,
   But on t'other side of the water.'

As she told the pathetic story of the doomed courtship of the Ratcatcher's daughter the seller of lily-vite sand, Charlie's eyes were fixed on her face, following every word until the Ratcatcher's daughter had been accidentally drowned in the bottom of the dirty Thames, to the inconsolable grief of her adorer.

'So he cut his froat wiv a square of glass,
   And stabbed his donkey arter,
And that vos the end of Lily-vite sand,
   His donkey and the Ratcatcher's daughter.'

The baby's eyes were closed. Was he asleep? Tentatively she began to withdraw her hand. At once the eyes opened. 'C'emmy, C'emmy!' he wailed. A church clock nearby tolled six. Marianne looked mute appeal at her daughter. Clemence gave her a reassuring grin.

' 'S all right, Mum. I won't go tonight.'

She was not to go the next night, nor the next, nor for weeks. Charlie recovered very slowly, and clung to his sister as to a rock in the stormy sea of his young life. Her only chance of going out, except to run errands, was when the finer days came and she could wander down to the Olympic while Charlie slept through the afternoon, and watch rehearsals. Dad, she thought, was not as good an actor as Mr. Willard, or even Mr. Boleyn or Mr. Cross. He was given speaking parts now, but they were very small ones and tended to be low-life characters. Miss Hewitt's lessons had improved his voice, but you could still hear i's, o's and a's that sounded wrong, though Clemence couldn't have said why. Loving and loyal, she was sad for him.

Miss Hewitt, too, was unhappy about her protégé. With looks like his the man ought to have got beyond 'Me Lord, the carriage wites'. It was a pity and a waste. Perhaps she should turn her teaching gift towards the child, so much better material. She called Clemence into her office.

'Clemence, have you learned yet to read and write?'

Clemence's lips drooped. 'No, Miss Hewitt.'

'I see. You could go to school, of course . . .'

'Oh no! Mum can't spare me! She's not well, and there's Charlie.'

Miss Hewitt privately thought that she would like to give Mum a piece of her mind. The woman would have been better employed spending her pregnancy in teaching her daughter the Three R's, than sitting about feeling sorry for herself.

'Would you like me to teach you?'

Clemence gasped. 'Oh, yes, please! Would you, Miss Hewitt? Then I could play proper parts and – and learn to be a lady, like.'

Miss Hewitt flipped through her book of engagements. 'How would you like to come to my house on Sunday, if your mother can spare you for the day, and we will begin?

An omnibus will bring you all the way to Brompton.'

Clemence was sure her mother would be able to spare her, with Dad being at home. 'And will Sheba be there?'

The spaniel, hearing her name, came to Clemence and laid her chin confidingly on the child's knee, looking up with that expression of sentimental yearning tinged with sorrow peculiar to spaniels. Clemence wasn't sure whether she was looking forward to Sunday more because of the lesson or because she would be with Sheba, all day.

Miss Hewitt's home was the grandest Clemence had ever seen. A tall stuccoed house in a terrace, it wore an air of impeccable respectability without ostentation. Standing in the handsome portico Clemence felt very small and, for her, a little nervous.

Sheba's basket was in the huge kitchen, by the open range. She had a blue cushion to lie on and a little tartan blanket ('just like the Queen's dogs at Balmoral' said Miss Hewitt) and china dishes for her food. Clemence was as much impressed by the kitchen as by a glimpse of the imposing drawing-room, a vision of crimson velvet curtains and crystal chandelier. She had never seen, or imagined, such a kitchen, brought up as she had been in a living-room with a little hob-grate. Dazedly she looked round at the ceiling-high dressers, their shelves filled with neatly-ranged plates of many colours, and fat, smooth jugs. There were racks of spotlessly clean pans, and of shining things of brass and copper for which she couldn't imagine any use; and the range was a wonderful thing of ovens, boiling-rings, bars for holding kettles, compartments for heating plates and dishes, grills and hobs, and a steady-glowing fire animating the whole structure. From the oven came a most delicious smell of roasting meat. Saliva rushed into Clemence's mouth. A very large lady addressed by Miss Hewitt as Mrs. Blore, who was mixing something in a huge basin, caught the hungry look on the child's face.

'Would the little girl like a biscuit, madam?' she asked. 'I've a batch just out of the oven.' Clemence's gaze automatically went to one of Sheba's feeding-dishes conspicuously labelled BISCUITS, at which Miss Hewitt and Mrs. Blore laughed.

'Not dog-biscuits, dear,' said Mrs. Blore, offering her a plate full of tempting golden crispy rounds. They were hot to the touch and hotter to the mouth, but Clemence accepted them eagerly. 'Can I give Sheba a bit, please?' she asked.

'Sheba eats far too much as it is,' Miss Hewitt said. 'But as a Sunday treat she may have a small piece.' Clemence knelt by the basket and felt immensely privileged when Sheba graciously condescended to snap up the offering, and rise from her basket in the expectation of more.

'No, that's quite enough,' said her mistress reprovingly. 'You will get much too fat. Come along, Clemence; you must come and visit Sheba again in summer, when she has her puppies!'

Puppies! a basketful of tiny fat miniature Shebas! Clemence was rapt at the thought. Somehow, those moments in the kitchen stayed in her mind more than any other memory of that day. She remembered, but vaguely, sitting in a big room with a lot of books in it, copying the letters Miss Hewitt was writing down so carefully for her, A, B, C, D, E, all neatly arranged between ruled lines with thick down-strokes and thin upstrokes. She would have been able to attend better if the surroundings had not been quite so awe-some. At midday Miss Hewitt's parents arrived home from church; she was brought out of the Libery, as the book-room seemed to be called, to curtsey to a delicate-looking elderly lady in a black silk dress that rustled, and a bonnet with velvet violets on top, and to an old gentleman with a beard who smiled kindly and shook Clemence's hand. Then she was given her own luncheon in the Libery, though she'd much rather have had it downstairs with Mrs. Blore and Sheba. A maid in a starched cap and apron brought it to her on a tray; it was delicious, meat and roast potatoes and a vegetable Clemence had never tasted before, and a beautiful pudding with jam at the bottom and crisped egg-white, like a range of little snowy mountains, at the top.

After the meal Clemence was so sleepy that the afternoon lesson went rather badly.

'Well, Clemence,' and Miss Hewitt laid down her pen with a certain relief, 'we'll have to try another day. Now, take home this exercise-book, and copy the letters over and over again. You'll soon learn.'

But Clemence didn't. The next day her mother fell into labour. The household was chaos once more, Clemence and Charlie banished downstairs to Mrs. Johnson, while Mrs. Pigge, temporarily without a baby of her own at the breast, moved in to look after Marianne.

Clemence was telling Charlie his bedtime story, a saga of fairies and giants, when her father appeared, coated and hatted. 'Come on,' he ordered her sharply, 'time we went.'

'Where to, Dad?'

'Where d'you think? I've got a living to earn and mouths to feed, haven't I?'

Clemence looked at him in surprise. He had not been his cheerful self, lately; she supposed it was because he got such poor parts. But now he looked cross and sour, as Mr. Boleyn looked when the ghost walked on Fridays and he got less in his pay-packet than he'd expected. 'I thought you'd be staying with Mama,' she said.

'Then you can think again. Your grandma and Mrs. P. have got *her* in charge. You'll be better off at the theatre than hanging about here.' Clemence was about to say 'But it isn't my night,' when she thought better of it. For some reason Dad needed her, more than Mum did, or Charlie, who had dozed off. She nodded, and tiptoed out to Mr. and Mrs. Johnson, who were having their tea.

'Charlie's asleep, and Dad wants me to go with him. Is it all right?'

'Bless you love, o'course,' said Mrs. Johnson. 'I'll go up if anybody's wanted. And so will Mr. J. if there's errands to be run, for in spite of being on his feet all day he's ever willing to go forth into the wilderness. Smile upon those you meet on the way up the ladder of life, I always say, and it'll be writ down in the Book against your name.' She resumed her fried mussels, while Mr. Johnson, with two more collections to make that night, smiled palely.

The walk to the Olympic was not as cheerful as usual. Albert was silent, for him. Clemence whistled *Tommy make room for your Uncle*, in which her father usually joined, but he told her irritably to shut it. They walked so fast that they arrived in Wych Street nearly half an hour early. Albert turned into the Queen of Bohemia, Clemence at his heels. She had never been in the place before; after the curtain other men in the company would go there, but her father always took her straight home. He must be known there, however, she thought, for the lady behind the counter called him Albert and seemed to know what he wanted before he ordered it. It was gin, and Clemence disliked the smell of it.

'Come on, little 'un, what'll you take?' said the lady, who had a lot of bright pinkish hair and a very low bodice with a frill round it.

'Cocoa, please,' Clemence replied, to the immense amusement of those present. Her father told her to cut along, and she went, gladly, for the place smelt horrible. At home they had beer for supper sometimes, and hot punch at Christmas, but nothing else. Clemence had heard a lot of jokes about drinking, but so far they had meant nothing to her.

At the theatre she was still too early. Only the stage staff were there, the men who looked after the gas footlights and the properties. She went into a dressing-room, and wandered about, idly reading the good-luck messages stuck round the looking-glass, playing with the hare's foot on the dressing-table, experimentally applying pink powder to her face with it and red greasepaint to her mouth. Yes, the effect was striking, better than grandma's rouge.

'Charming! quite charming!' said a voice behind her. It was Mr. Gwynne, an elderly actor who generally played faithful old retainers, irate fathers and cruel landlords. He was a small, thinnish man with sparse hair and a mouth which unaccountably reminded Clemence of worms. He was not one of her favourites, but she smiled at him. 'I was seeing how I looked,' she said. Mr. Gwynne shut the door behind him.

'You look like a very pretty young lady. Very pretty. And very young. I like young ladies, you know. How old are you, my dear?'

'Nearly seven, sir.'

'Well, well. Sweet seven without the teen, and never been kissed.' He was advancing on her with a curious look in his eye. 'Oh, but I have –' she began, only to find herself gripped in a tight hold, and Mr. Gwynne's wormlike lips on hers, writhing against them, while his hand was pulling up her skirts and fumbling with the tops of her stockings. 'Nice, nice, nice little girl,' he was crooning, 'shall we see how soft and tender a nice little girl can be?' His fingers had found what they were seeking, and Clemence gave a shriek that would have done credit to Mrs. Siddons. Somehow she managed to drag a hand free and claw at the face so sickeningly pressed against hers. Mr. Gwynne jumped back.

'You little baggage! We must have a smack for that, mustn't we!' He had her across his knee, tearing at the tapes that held her knickers, while she struggled and kicked and screamed. 'Oh, don't, don't! Oh, please, somebody!'

With a slow squeak the door swung open. Mr. Gwynne hastily abandoned his explorations, giving Clemence the chance to slip off his knee. In the corridor, framed by the doorway, stood a lady. She was nobody Clemence had ever seen before, but something about her proclaimed the actress. She was not young, but very beautiful still, with dark hair just greying in ringlets framing her face, her shoulders and bosom almost bare but for a glittering necklace, her slender waist seeming slenderer for the frills of crinoline that framed it. She said nothing, the stern glance of her dark eyes expressing more than words. Mr. Gwynne gave a violent shiver, pushing Clemence away from him. With a muttered exclamation he almost ran out of the room.

'Thank you –' Clemence began. But the strange lady was no longer at the door. Perhaps she'd followed Mr. Gwynne after he had pushed so rudely past her. She was nowhere to

70

be seen in the corridor, or on the flight of dank stone steps that led down to the stage. One or two supers, straggling in, said nobody had passed them. Clemence made her way to Fred's workroom. He and a young assistant were repairing a flat representing part of a woodland glade, through which somebody had clumsily stuck a spear.

'What's up, Little Miss Moffat?' Fred enquired kindly. Clemence subsided on a tea-chest. 'It's all right, Fred. Just that I wanted to thank the lady, only I can't find her.'

'What lady was that? I thought we only kept actresses here.' He winked at his assistant. Clemence got out her story, blushing and stumbling over the part of it which concerned Mr. Gwynne's attentions. Fred motioned his assistant to get on with something else, for the boy's eyes appeared on the point of popping out of his head. He listened in silence to Clemence, puffing at his clay pipe. Then he said:

'Now, Miss Moffatt, you take a bit advice from an old 'un. Next time any b – any chap tries to take liberties like that with you (and they will try, young as you are) this is what you've got to do.' He demonstrated the effectiveness of a knee applied to the tenderest part of the male anatomy. 'Keep your nails sharp and your eyes about you, and remember, the older they are the dirtier. (Nay, don't look at me, lass, I'm noan that sort.) You were right lucky this time, but next time there mightn't be any lady.'

Clemence pondered. 'Do you think she'll be in front tonight, Fred?'

'Shouldn't wonder,' Fred grunted. 'Friend of the management, mebbe. Now, I've nowt here for you, so cut off to Wardrobe and get busy with your needle.'

When she had gone he went to the corner where he kept his personal belongings, and took down from the wall a small framed print. Under the unflattering gaslight the face of the subject smiled flirtatiously. A necklace of jewels sparkled on her bosom. Her crinoline hem was raised to show a pair of elegant sandalled feet in the first position of dancing.

'Thirty years dead,' he said to the portrait. 'Thirty years

71

dead, Eliza Vestris. Queen of the old Olympic, you was. Queen of Hearts too, and mine among 'em. Why is it never me you come to: old Fred, as used to be young Fred, worshipping the ground you walked on? Was it to save the little lass you come tonight?'

He hung the print back on its nail and, shaking his white head, went back to his work.

When Albert Moffat's youngest child Sophia was a week old he was sacked by the Olympic management for drunkenness. The taint of alcohol on his breath had not escaped Agnes Hewitt's attention, but she had overlooked it because of his domestic trials. When it came to the first night of the new drama, *To the Death*, Albert, as footman, was required to knock, enter, and deliver a telegram on a tray to Miss Florence West, who, stately in an upright chair, awaited it. The first intimation of Albert's entry was a resounding hiccup, followed by Albert himself, his wig on askew, a vacant smile on his face. He paused, teetering, then advanced on Miss West, seeming uncertain of her exact location on the stage. A growl of 'Get *on*!' from the prompt corner jerked him into activity. 'Thish – thish telly,' he began. Miss West held out her hand imperiously. 'Well, sir, give it to me!' she improvised. Albert turned, tripped on the square of carpet covering the boards, and like a ball from a cannon shot forward into the fireplace. It was only a thing of cardboard and paint: Albert disappeared through it head first, in the manner of the Clown's dog jumping through a paper hoop, and remained there, kicking, his head and shoulders where the chimney-flue might be supposed to be.

The curtain was rung down and the scene re-played from the beginning. But this time Albert made no appearance, and the damaged fireplace flat had been hidden from view by a screen.

He got his notice within half an hour. 'I am very sorry, Mr. Moffat,' said Miss Hewitt. 'I have overlooked much, but this is beyond endurance.'

'Couldn't you give me one more chance?' he pleaded, sober now.

'I could, out of consideration for your little daughter, if nothing else. But I shall shortly be handing over the management of the Olympic to Mr. Yorke Stephens, and in all honesty I cannot load on him a drunken actor. Again, I am sorry. Goodnight.'

For the last time he went out through the stage door, his feet dragging, his hand touching the wage-envelope in his pocket as though it were the only reality in the world.

CHAPTER SIX

'Help!' A woman's scream ripped into the dank air of Whitechapel. Drinkers heard it in the flashy gin-palaces, and ran out to see what was doing. Children, still playing in the streets and courts in winter dusk lifted their lice-infested heads to listen, while their ragged mothers, in tenement rooms high above them, opened cracked windows the better to hear.

'It's Jack the Ripper!' they were telling each other. ''e's claimed Another Victim!' They buzzed with excitement, an ants' nest disturbed. But nobody offered to investigate the cause of the screaming. It was only a few weeks before, on November 9, that the body of Mary Kelly, an Irish prostitute, had been found at her lodging in Miller's Court mutilated with a fiendish savagery which outdid the Ripper's previous efforts. At midnight she had been heard singing *Only a violet I plucked for my mother's grave*; at 10.30 next morning a rent-collector had found her corpse in a state from which even police-surgeons flinched. Since then, the area round Miller's Court had been a place of hideous fascination for those who had read the awful details in the Penny Illustrated Paper.

At Drury Lane Dan Leno was causing immense mirth by his impersonation of the Wicked Aunt in pantomime. In Parliament Mr. Gladstone, of all men, was being accused of immorality, a charge arising from his misunderstood zeal for helping fallen women. Down at Portsmouth, young Dr. Arthur Conan Doyle was writing his second novel, *The Sign of the Four*, about a detective called Sherlock Holmes. It was to be published in *Lippincott's Magazine*, for which the fashionable author Oscar Wilde was writing *The Picture of Dorian Gray*. And in an ancient Thames-side inn near Oxford Jerome Klapka Jerome was laughing as he wrote a light-hearted story of a river trip, *Three Men in a Boat*.

While all these interesting and civilised things were taking place, the Moffat family was living in squalid discomfort. After Albert's dismissal, which had automatically brought Clemence's in its wake, the Clerkenwell rooms had become impossibly expensive.

They were one less now, for Harriet Dumas was dead. She had come home one night and sat down without her usual humorous remarks about her poor feet. Her face was a curious colour and she spoke only with an effort. Alarmed, Marianne insisted that she should go to bed, and was even more alarmed when she meekly agreed.

Once there, she lay unmoving and limp. No, there was nothing she wanted. It would be silly to call the doctor. A sudden change in her face made Marianne cry out with fear. She bent over her mother; the heavy eyes opened, and with a ghost of her old smile Harriet said. 'It's the Duke, love. Come for me at last . . .' With a last effort, her eyes moved to the violin on the wall, and it was not for the Duke that her face lit up before she fell back against her daughter's shoulder.

Death had spared her something, for the family soon moved away from the pleasant old house to lodgings in Black Lion Yard, Whitechapel. The new accommodation consisted of one moderately-sized room with a tiny scullery off it. A trickle of cold water came from a rusty tap, the one 'convenience', an earth closet, was in the yard at the back; it served the six families who lived in the house, and was never less than disgusting. The cellars below, where Mr. O'Rourke the landlord kindly allowed his tenants to keep their small stocks of coal, literally crawled with cockroaches, a black shiny sea of living loathesomeness. The Moffats' own room housed brown things in the wainscot which paid no rent, while enjoying all the amenities of home life; they were not desirable as co-lodgers, but compared with the cockroaches they made agreeable pets. Clemence was sometimes sent down to the cellar for coal when her father was out. It was a nightmare experience she would have given anything to avoid, and for years it came back to her in actual nightmare form.

When Albert realised what had happened to him he went on a drinking bout which put him in bed for two days, and horrified Marianne so much that she could scarcely bring herself to speak to him. Tears and reproaches were her weapons when she did.

'Call yourself clever? I thought you were going to be Lord High Everything at the Olympic, the way you talked. And look at you now, a drunken beast that can't buy his own children bread but must have as much of his own nasty spirits as he likes! How are we going to live, tell me that?'

At first Albert shut his ears to her and sat in sulky silence. When this provoked her even further he was goaded into speech.

'And you call yourself a wife, do you? What have *you* done to feed the kids, except take in bits of tatting? I'm sick of you, I am, sitting on your backside all day, watching that child work for you and bring up the others for you, while you give yourself fine-lady airs and go on about your health. You're as well as I am.'

'I'm *not*!' she tearfully retorted. 'God knows what I've suffered bearing your children, not to mention losing my mother. But men are all the same, selfish unfeeling brutes.'

Then she would relapse into sobs, rocking herself on the edge of the chair in the age-old female way of grieving, while Albert swore to himself and lit a pipe with trembling hands.

'There you go – smoking! when I can't afford so much as –'

Albert's patience was at an end. He gave her a ringing slap on the side of the head, making her stagger. She burst into hysterical tears, bringing a fusillade of knocks on the ceiling from the tenant upstairs. Albert flung himself down beside her and took her in his arms, where she lay weakly snuffling against his shirt-front.

'There, there, love, I didn't mean to do it. Honest I didn't.

Never hit you before, have I, and I won't again. There, quiet now, my pretty girl . . .'

Only, thought Clemence sadly, under the shelter of her blanket on her mattress-bed, Mum wasn't a pretty girl any more. She was beginning to look like the other women of Whitechapel, far older than she was, with deep lines across her forehead and the nose-to-mouth corners, and her brown hair had lost its shine. Neither she nor Dad ever looked quite clean nowadays; which wasn't surprising, because none of them *were* clean, even though they hadn't yet got Things in their hair like other people in the neighbourhood, and went to the Public Baths once a week. Everything that could be pawned had gone to 'Uncle' – the cupid with the hearts, the silver crucifix, even the lovely Chelsea china dog Albert had given Clemence to make up for parting with Sheba.

When the food position got really desperate, Albert and Clemence would go along to the London Hospital up the road and wait for the scraps of food given out at the back door to the local poor. It was deeply humiliating, even to the child, and the food, though welcome, was usually cold and stale. But 'Never say die!' and 'Good luck's just around the corner' Albert would say, cocking his hat at an angle to make Clemence laugh. She would never forget how he taught her to meet misfortune, poor, weak, unlucky Dad.

Exhausted, after a bout of crying, Marianne had sobbed herself off to sleep in her husband's arms. Gently he laid her down on the bed and put a coat over her. Then he came over to Clemence, and sat on the mattress beside her.

'What are we going to do, Clem?'

She stroked his hand. 'Poor Dad.'

'D'you know, I've thought more than once of putting my pride in my pocket, and asking my father for a bit of help. Then I've remembered things he's said, and thought better of it.'

'Oh, why don't you go? If you tell him about Mum, and the babies –'

Albert shook his head. 'You don't know him, darlin'. He's

77

a hard man. When I married your Mum he shut the door in my face, and I've never set eyes on him since.'

But he did go, back to Rosoman Street, neatly dressed and looking as much like a respectable clerk and as little like an actor as he could. After he had knocked three times he saw a corner of lace curtain in the front window cautiously lifted and replaced. Then the door was opened. His father stood there, seeming smaller than last time they'd met. He had gone almost bald, a few scraps of iron-grey hair straggling above his temples. His face had set into deep lines of disillusion and bitterness. He and Albert regarded each other in silence. Albert broke it.

'Well, Father. Aren't you going to ask me in?'

The old man stood immobile in the doorway.

'What have you come for?' he asked, without expression or emotion.

'To see you and mother, and – have a talk.'

His father smiled sourly. 'You've learnt fine speech. That'll have come wi' play-acting. What else has come w't? Honour and riches, the power and the glory?'

'No. At least, I've not done badly. But it takes time – and I've got three children . . .'

His father broke in triumphantly. 'Aha! I thought that'd be it. You've come cap in hand like the Prodigal, you've arisen and come to your father, saying, Father, I have sinned, and am no more worthy to be called thy son. Is that the way of it?'

Albert felt his temper rising, in the old familiar way, at his father's mockery. 'No, that's not the way of it. I thought you'd the right to know we were in want. Through my fault, I grant you that, but . . .' He knew from the malicious look on his father's face that if he went on he would be led into a string of lame phrases, each of which would be demolished by a biting rejoinder from the Scriptures. That had always been the way, and it always would be.

'All right,' he said, 'so you don't care if I end up in a spunging-house for debt and the wife and kids go begging. I wasn't going to ask you for much. Can I see Mother?'

78

In answer the old man barred the doorway, arms out-spread, silently daring his son to push him aside. It would have been easy, but force of habit stayed the son's hand. He moved too late, and the door was slammed in his face. Before it shut he thought he caught a glimpse, in the lobby, of a little bent form hovering in the shadows.

He walked up Rosoman Street, on his old courting route. There were other theatres besides the Olympic. He was sober now, and presentable. At the stage door of Sadler's Wells he asked to see the manager, and was given an interview after a half-hour wait. He had barely uttered ten words before the manager told him politely but crisply that there were no vacancies in the company, none at all.

Three other theatres returned the same answer; the fourth was closed for re-decoration. At the fifth, the Park in Camden Town, the stage-doorkeeper suggested that if Albert were to try farther east he might do better. Weary and footsore, Albert spent two of the precious pence from his last wages on a tram-ride which spared him a mile or two of walking. Bleakly he stared out of the tram window at the hurrying people in the streets, the advertisements for Row-lands' Macassar Oil and Sugg's Celebrated Gas Burners; at spanking high-stepping horses and weary thin-ribbed ones harnessed to cabs. His whole soul longed for a very stiff drink, repeated until the familiar blessed cloud of euphoria descended on him and wrapped him safe from worries.

But when he reached Whitechapel Road and the Pavilion Theatre, to which his friend had directed him, he managed by immense force of will to pass the door of the pub close by.

For his virtue, he was rewarded. The Pavilion was putting on a Shakespeare season. Shakespeare being addicted to large casts, a number of walking gentlemen and ladies were required, and he would be taken on forthwith, said Mr. Abrahams, the manager.

Mr. Morris Abrahams was, as his name suggested, a Jew. More people were than not, in Whitechapel. He had worked in the theatre all his life, as everything from callboy upwards.

At one time he had been manager of the East London theatre, where plays in Yiddish were given for the gratification of the locals, all with Jewish heroes and Gentile villains. Out of this, and other ventures, he had done very well, as the rotundities of his figure and his rubicund face suggested. He looked like a Semitic Mr. Pickwick; the diamonds in his tie-pin were real, and the watch-chain slung across his ample stomach was of 22-carat gold. His voice was rich and booming, with an exotic quality, his eyes were dark and languorous.

'So,' he was saying to Albert, 'as from Monday, you'll be with us, my boy. It's a good theatre, a very good theatre, my Pavilion. Work, boy, work, and you may rise to the top of the tree. Look at me: I worked. Here I am, in me own chair, in me own office, in me own theatre. Look at my brothers: one's a tailor, t'other's a pawnbroker. They didn't work. Moral clear.'

Albert agreed, thanked Mr. Abrahams, and rose to leave. On the point of doing so he asked if the manager knew any cheap but clean lodgings nearby, suitable for his wife and family. Mr. Abrahams put the tips of his fingers together and seemed to be communing with some Jehovan house-agent.

'I do,' he finally pronounced. 'At 10 Black Lion Yard there are rooms to let. They may not be nice rooms: I haven't seen 'em but I should hazard that they're not, on the whole, nice. Cheap, however, they are, and the landlord's known to me – O'Rourke by name – and to my knowledge there's been no trouble there.'

'Trouble?'

'Police. Knife-fighting. Women using rooms as a brothel – that kind of thing.'

'Oh, ah,' said Albert, with mixed relief and apprehension. It had not occurred to him to imagine the existence of 'that kind of thing' in connection with his home.

For that, despite the inappropriateness of the word, was what the squalid room would be, for himself and his family.

It would be pleasant to record that under the benevolent

rule of Mr. Abrahams Albert resumed the broken thread of his career and pursued a tranquil course towards fame and fortune. But the truth is otherwise. The work itself was no strain. His journey to and from the theatre was nothing to that between Clerkenwell and the Olympic. But the stresses of his domestic life were too much for him. Not the least of them was that, with only one room for all of them, Marianne refused to let him make love to her, however fast asleep the children appeared to be on their small mattresses.

'Clemence might *hear*,' she hissed at him.

'Got to learn some time, hasn't she?'

'Sssh! The child's not eight yet. Do you want to shock her into fits?'

Take a lot to do that with our Clem, thought her father, turning a surly back on his wife.

Not surprisingly, sexual pleasure being refused at home, he sought it elsewhere. In the Pavilion company was a young lady calling herself Juliet Huntly. She was in her early twenties, petite and pretty, with enough Jewish blood in spite of the Huntly to give a becoming dark sparkle to her eye and a damask quality to her complexion. Nor was Albert's fair manliness unpleasing to her. She had a room nearby, an attic room, like the nest of a particularly seductive bird, where there were tables and chairs upholstered in lush green satin, a pleasingly feminine aura of rosewater and powder, and a small but adequate half-tester bed.

Albert ceased to beg for his wife's favours.

Clemence had a rare faculty for being awake while seeming asleep, and some passages in the plays she had acted in and seen had not been meaningless to her. She noticed that there were no more soft scuffles and kissing sounds from her parents' bed: that there were not even any arguments, only an untender Goodnight and a cold silence. Dad was looking unusually pleased with himself. One morning she saw him buy a bunch of flowers from an old woman and stick one in his buttonhole. The flowers were not brought home; she said nothing to her mother about them.

One evening, Albert came home from an afternoon rehearsal looking flushed and exhilarated. Marianne was sewing by the fire, Clemence getting the little ones ready for bed. Albert bestowed kisses upon them all. As he straightened up from embracing Marianne, she surveyed his waistcoat critically, and refastened the two top buttons.

'What's up?' he asked.

'Costume rehearsal today?' She was still sewing calmly.

'N– yes,' he corrected himself quickly.

'Bring the mirror, Clemence. Yes, off the wall.' Clemence gave it to her, and she handed it to Albert. 'Costume and make-up too, was it?' Nervous, he surveyed his reflection, turning the mirror this way and that. The light from their dingy window was not dazzling, but he (and Clemence) could see quite clearly a heart-shaped pink impression on the corner of his jaw.

'Well, yes,' he said in that frankly ingenuous tone which only goes with lies, 'some of the girls *were* trying out a few colours . . .'

Marianne sprang to her feet. 'Liar! I was round at the theatre this afternoon, asking for you. George told me the rehearsal finished at two. So where were you trying out colours, then?' Her own colours were the twin red flags in her cheeks.

Albert looked as if he were going to cry. 'Look, love, it was just a –'

Marianne seized Clemence by the hand, scooped up Charlie and the baby, and propelled them out of the room. Charlie began to cry. 'Want Mum! Want Dad!' As always when he was upset, his face became suffused, a bluish-purple, and he began to choke. Clemence clasped him to her, lowering herself to the dirty oil-cloth covered floor so that she could hold the baby as well. From within their room the high hysterical voice of her mother was shrieking above the raised voice of her husband. Clemence's mouth turned down. Even she was beginning to crack. Downstairs the front door slammed, as it was always doing in that human warren. Tired-sounding footsteps ascending the stairs drove the tears back from Clemence's eyes. 'Stupid!' she scolded herself. 'Cry before people, I won't, that I won't.'

The arrival was a small, thin man of middle age, with something of the air of a friendly gnome. His bowler hat's brim was shiny with much raising, his body bent with long hours of maintaining the same position for hours at a time. Exposure to all weathers had not given his face a healthy glow, but had overlaid it with something almost like a suntan: for he was a London cab-driver, slave to any fare who hailed him, a puny David to the Goliath of omnibus drivers and those who steered tramcars on their relentless tracks.

''Ello, 'ello, 'ello!' said Sam Clickett, ''oom 'ave we 'ere? Why I do believe it's them nice-lookin' children as I've seen a-promenadin' rahnd the Jews' Cemetery and along the 'igh Street on a fine day.'

'Yes,' said Clemence, swallowing the last of the traitorous tears, 'I take the little ones out most days for Mum.'

'And what might you be a-doin' on the landin', which ain't the most agreeable of spots?' (Nor was it, for one corner of it was occupied by a drain installed long ago, in the house's comparatively prosperous days, for the use of maids emptying slops.)

'Keeping out of the way,' said Clemence with a wan smile. 'There's a row goin' on in there –' jerking her head towards the door. Sam listened. 'Rah! I should say there is. Come on, let's go and see if it's quieter upstairs: Peace with Honour, as Lord Beaconsfield remarked.' He led the way, Sophy in his arms for once not expressing displeasure at being carried by a stranger.

The Clicketts lived on the floor above, across the landing. Sam opened the door and shouted 'Bella!' To Clemence's nostrils there came a scent which was in its own way as agreeable as the ineffable smell of Theatre. The basis of it was in a stockpot suspended from a hook over the fire; a magic cauldron in which lurked the essences of meat, poultry, vegetables, giving out their blended savour to the room. Other odours were those of baking bread, and hay. The room was in a state of cheerful disorder, everything strewn everywhere. A pretty girl of about sixteen was laying a table, a younger one stirring the broth, and a small child who might be of either sex was sitting squarely on a rag rug before the fire, thoughtfully emptying a tin of sand over its yellow curls.

'Bella!' called Sam again, and was answered by a melodious sound like a street-cry. Into the room came a large woman who might have posed for Britannia on the coin. Ample, majestic, her figure disdained stays. Across her spreading bosom a blouse only just managed to stay fastened by the aid of a safety-pin. Her rich auburn hair, with a sprinkling of pepper-and-salt in it, was gathered back in a careless knot, her handsome face was one smile.

'Ducky' said the beautiful slattern, gathering Sam to her bosom. 'Late again. And wot 'ave you been and found?' surveying the three children.

Without uttering a word, Sam conveyed in the silent shorthand used by long-married couples that there was trouble downstairs, and that these were refugees from it.

'Well!' exclaimed his wife, brawny arms akimbo, 'there's a fine thing. Three more to supper withaht notice. Never mind, the more the merrier. I must say, that little perisher looks peaky, don't 'e, and that baby wants changin', I can tell from 'ere. Give it over –' taking Sophy professionally from Sam's arms and casually tucking her under one of her own while she ran her hand through Charlie's hair. 'Clean, though, thank Gawd. Can't be doin' with nits.'

'You mustn't mind the missis,' Sam told the staring Clemence. 'She speaks her mind, she does. Some gets shirty abaht it, but I can tell *you* wouldn't, darlin'.' Clemence smiled back. No, she wouldn't get shirty. She sensed a kindness in these people which would prove a refuge to her and hers in this place where unhappiness, she knew, would come to the Moffat family. Bella drew her in, and shut the door.

The supper they all shared had trotters as its principal delicacy, and bread with the new butter substitute, margarine, washed down with a pot of heady orange-coloured tea (Bella had a 'eavy 'and with the ladle, Sam correctly told

84

Clemence). When their first hunger was satisfied Bella enquired of Sam. 'All right today, is 'e?'

Sam, his mouth full, nodded. 'Ate 'is dinner a treat,' he said indistinctly. 'Went orf twenty minutes or so, on the rank. Seem to do 'im good.'

'And 'is legs?'

Sam shook his head sadly. 'Poorish. Back to the bandages tomorrer.'

'Strengthenin', that's wot 'e needs,' said Bella. 'I've got a bowl o' mutton jelly you can take 'im before 'e goes to bed. That ought to put 'air on 'is chest. 'Ere, look at Little Blue-eyes, the 'uman question-mark! Who d'you think we're talkin' abaht, eh?'

'Your granddad?' hazarded Clemence. Both Clicketts roared with laughter, joined by Polly and Amy, while Baby Vicky beat on the edge of the table with her spoon.

'Granddad! That's ripe, that is,' said Sam, wiping his eyes. 'It's a nag, love, a 'orse. I drives a cab, see, and Inkerman's all in all to me. One of the family, is Inkerman.'

Bella explained. 'Sam's 'ad Inkerman since 'e were a foal. Fahnd 'im at the slaughter'ouse.' Ignoring Sam's silencing gestures, she went on: 'Sam 'ere was on 'is way across Smithfield when 'e sees this knacker (that's a 'orse-killer, love) wiv a little fing in 'is arms as Sam thought were a dog. "Want an 'orse, cheap?" this knacker says, and Sam says, "Get on, that ain't no 'orse." "Strite, it is," saws the knacker. "It's muvver come in 'ere for slaughter an' I see right off she's in foal and not far orf 'aving it. So I smuggles 'er aht into a shed at the back and she 'as it, and dies, 'cause she was an old lady. But I saves the foal and I don't want to see it die. Can't tike it 'ome meself, got nowhere to put it."'

'And *I* replies,' said Sam, ' "Give you five bob and tike it 'ome to the missis," and 'e says "Done", and I wraps the bleedin' little fing up and brings it to Bella, and she welcomes this foal like 'e was a little biby.'

'And 'ere 'e is, to this very day, in the mews, just across Brick Lane in Chicksand Street.'

'Why is he called Ink – what you said?' asked Clemence.

'Cause I saw service in the Crimean War, my love,' said Sam. 'I fought at Alma and Balaclava and Inkerman, and it left me only fit to be a cabbie. I got one leg crooked, see,' and he demonstrated the twisted angle of a sparrow-like limb.

'You haven't got a dog, have you?' Clemence asked.

'Dawg? Bless you, no. Inkerman's enough.'

'Can – can I see him, please?'

'Course you can. Come along o' me when I puts 'im to bed.'

Charlie, who had been following the conversation closely, immediately broke into a wail of 'Want horsey! Want see horsey!' until efficiently hushed by Bella, with specious promises of a wooden 'un.

Inkerman was never likely to win the Derby. He was a rusty brown with a little white streak down his nose, and in build he resembled the barrel-shaped horses of Stubbs and Morland more than the 1889 variety. But to Clemence he was a thing of radiant loveliness. Of kind disposition, he bent his long head graciously down, that she might pat him the more easily. His eyes were brown and tender, his lashes as thick and black as any beauty's. Bella had made up a compound which was smeared round them to prevent his being pestered by flies. He and his stall smelt sweet, of things Clemence had hardly heard of, but sensed instinctively: daisy-meadows, hayricks, streams that ran between willows, all that made up The Country.

She was allowed to hold the bowl of mutton jelly, and afterwards the mug of half-and-half which Bella had recommended, beer being good for man and beast.

Inkerman tucked up, as it were, for the night, Clemence accompanied Sam back home. When they reached the landing she listened, apprehensively. Behind the door everything was quiet. She opened it softly and peered in. Her mother was in bed, her face invisible. Sam, one arm round Clemence's shoulders, listened.

'Asleep,' he whispered. 'Come on. Better leave her. You stay with us.'

The Moffat children returned home next morning. The only signs of the fracas of the night before were a broken jug and a plant knocked to the floor. Marianne's eyes were red, but she was not to be drawn into conversation. 'Your Dad's at the theatre,' was all she would say in answer to questions. She seemed uninterested in Clemence's account of the people upstairs, and of the wonderful horse and Mr. Clickett having been a real soldier, and seen Miss Florence Nightingale.

That night Clemence, who had been up to visit the Clicketts again by invitation, was surprised to see her mother kneeling in front of a chair. On it was a doll Clemence had never seen before, with a black face and bright clothes. Her mother seemed to be talking to it, as though it could hear. When the door shut she jumped up with flaming cheeks.

'Don't you dare creep up behind me like that!' she shouted. 'Get yourself some supper and go to bed, at once.' When Clemence had undressed she came to say goodnight. The doll had gone, and the chair was back in place.

CHAPTER SEVEN

It was inevitable that Albert should eventually get the sack for drunkenness. After he had appeared, wavering, as Bernardo on the battlements of Elsinore, with a slow and scrupulous enunciation of his words and a tendency to shut his eyes when someone else was delivering a speech, Mr Abrahams sent for him, and addressed him, more in sorrow than in anger, but with firm purpose.

'You nearly got the bird last night, Mr. Moffat. Now I don't like my actors to get the bird. I'm very sorry, but you will have to go.'

Albert was shocked, stricken. To his protestations of reform and change of heart Mr. Abrahams listened patiently, before opening a drawer of his desk and counting out some coins.

'One week's money. Should you or yours be in trouble, apply to me. That I mean' (and he did) 'and I wish you well.' Albert was outside the door before the full impact of the interview registered with him. Then he took himself and his wages to the Black Lion.

The fortunes of the Moffats were in decline. The charms of Juliet Huntly ceased to be a threat to Marianne, possibly because of her prayer to the witch-doll but more probably because Miss Huntly very quickly lost interest in a lover with no money for presents. Albert got one or two engagements in local theatres: the little one in Wellclose Square, the Garrick in Leman Street. After losing them both he earned money wherever he could get it, and by whatever means. In the course of three years he became a shoeblack, a waiter, a holder of horses' heads at a pub (the nearest connection he was ever again to have with Shakespeare) and a shop assistant.

To the little money he earned was added what Marianne could make out of dressmaking. There was none to be had in the Whitechapel area, only work in the 'sweatshops' where girls and women wore their eyes out stitching garments which would be sold at West End prices, while the sewing-women got a few pence a day. Rather than do this, Marianne walked miles to better-class districts to put advertisements in shop-windows, or visit somebody who was known to be in want of a sempstress.

When Charlie was five he was sent to the Board School. There he was bullied and jeered at for his small size and timidity, his asthmatic paroxysms treated as deliberate. He was, not unnaturally, miserable.

'You didn't oughter send that child out,' Bella told Marianne. 'Choke 'isself into 'is grave, one day, 'e will.'

Marianne set her lips in a tight line, as she often did when receiving advice from Bella. 'There's nothing else for it,' she snapped. 'It's either that or starve.'

'Then let me take Sophy, and Clem can go to school.'

'I'll please myself, thank you.'

Bella looked speculatively after Marianne as she swept haughtily downstairs. There had been many evenings lately when she had seen Marianne and Albert going out, while the children were left alone. It had not taken much effort to work out where they were going. Conveniently near, at the corner of the High Road, more alluring than the Old Black Lion, was a 'gin palace' blazing with gas-light, the Mecca of the poor and the cheerless. So Milady had taken to the stuff, too, Bella reflected.

Clemence was only too well aware of her mother's lapse. Evening after evening she was left in charge of her sister and brother; getting them to sleep, doing what could be done to the room in the way of cleaning, and ignoring the brown things which came scuttering out of the skirting-board and from under the floor. It was a dreary time for her. Unable to read, even now (to her own shame), her only entertainment was watching the street. The flickering gaslight of winter made sinister shadows. Had the Ripper really ceased his dreadful campaign? People still talked of the victims found in a pool of their own blood, not a hundred yards away. The district was full of prostitutes. Would he strike again? Perhaps he would even come up the stairs in search of women . . . Clemence started as the front door slammed and steps began to climb the stairs. But no, it was only her mother and father. When they came in Dad would look flushed and sullen, unlike himself, and Mum, except for her unpainted face, might have been taken for one of the Ripper's intended victims. They'd start fighting, and Mum would even hit any child that happened to be awake and in her way; so Clemence used to cover the other two up and hide herself under the bed. More often than not it was she who got hit.

There was one night when a man knocked at the door and said he was an officer from the newly-formed Society for the Prevention of Cruelty to Children. He had been told, he said, of children's cries coming from the Moffats' room.

'Oh, no, sir,' said Clemence innocently. 'Couldn't have been any of us. It's them noises outside – you can't really tell where they're coming from.'

'Let's see your arms,' said the inspector. She dutifully rolled up her sleeves and displayed unblemished skin. (Lucky that bruise from the other night was higher up.) After an inspection of the other children he left, with a strong feeling that he had not seen everything.

But his visit brought home to Clemence the conviction that things couldn't go on like this any more. She prayed and prayed (though the Moffats never went to church now) to be shown the way to help all of them. 'Because only me can,' she said to herself. She knelt by her bed as she had done when she was a little girl, screwing her eyes tight shut and her hands together. 'Please, please,' she said to Somebody unknown: and waited for an answer.

It came, in a most improbable form; before her closed eyes floated a vision of Mr. Morris Abrahams, sitting in his office chair, as she'd seen him one day when Dad was at the Pavilion. What was it he'd said when he sacked Dad? 'Should you or yours be in trouble, come to me.' ('Fat lot of use saying that,' Albert had commented bitterly.)

She rose, put on her threadbare, outgrown coat, dragged

a comb through her rough curls, and set out. Her father was still asleep, heavy from the drinking of the night before; her mother had gone out taking Sophy, to deliver a lady's dress-making order. It was the ideal time.

At the Pavilion, the stage-door keeper seemed not to recognise her. Only her smile and the vivid blue eyes brought back the little girl who had occasionally accompanied her father to the theatre.

'Well, blow me down, it *is* Little Miss Moffat. You've grown into a young woman, my dear.' He surveyed appreciatively her plumply rounding figure.

'I'm thirteen, George, going on fourteen. Please, d'you think Mr. Abrahams would see me?' George scratched his head. 'I think he's got someone with him, but I'll see.' A minute later he was back with the news that Mr. Abrahams would receive her.

The Manager, a little more portly and with a little more grey in his black locks, reacted to her as George had done. A pretty, lively, well-grown girl, she deserved a better dress than that rag. She was not even clean, exuding a stuffiness which reminded Mr. Abrahams of the inside of an omnibus, a vehicle in which he no longer travelled. Her voice, when she began hesitantly to tell him of the family troubles, had reverted to pure Whitechapel, for she had a parrot ear for accents. What a pity, thought Mr. Abrahams, brought up in the old school of acting, when a player could be identified anywhere by his fruity, rolling Shakespeare Voice.

He listened patiently to her story. 'So you see, sir,' she was saying, 'we'll all be in the poor-'ouse, the way we're going. And as you told Dad you'd help . . .'

Mr. Abrahams meditated. 'I can't promise to take your father back, my dear; unless I am convinced that he has mended his ways.'

Clemence looked downcast.

'But,' he went on, 'if you're sure that he would make an effort to reform –'

'Oh yes, sir, he would!' she interrupted eagerly.

He held up a well-manicured hand. 'I had not finished,

my dear. I seem to recall that your father had a pleasant singing-voice. Would he be capable, do you think, of learning a few light popular ballads to be performed in public?'

Clemence was taken aback. In the old days Dad had been much given to warbling light popular ballads, and she had inherited his quick ear. But in public –?

'I think he'd try, sir, if it was something like that, and not beneath him like some of the things he's done. He's very proud, is Dad.'

'I ask,' said Mr. Abrahams, 'because a friend of mine, the manager of Belmont's Music Hall in Hackney Road, is looking for a light voice-and-piano turn for his bill. Now, before I recommend your father to go and see Mr. Cohen I shall want to see him myself.'

Albert was not anxious to see his old manager or Mr. Cohen. His confidence in himself was sapped by years of inactivity and by the fear of failure. He produced every argument possible. He was no singer, he couldn't read a note of music. His clothes were shabby. How could he face an audience, after so long away from the stage? The whole thing was ridiculous. So he went on, safe in the belief that Clemence would leave him alone.

He hadn't reckoned with his daughter. She was brushing the shoulders of his jacket, straightening his hair.

'Blimey, Dad, how you do talk,' she said. 'Come on, you look a treat.'

So it came about that Albert found himself on the stage of Belmont's Music Hall, giving twice-nightly renderings of songs at the piano to the accompaniment of Mr. Ernest de Navarro, a long-haired gentleman of gloomy disposition. He was an excellent pianist, with a melancholy cast of face which lent itself ideally to the romantic, mournful songs Albert usually sang. Albert was a tenor, and tenors were the natural singers of such ballads, so dear to the sentimental heart of the British public. In his sweet, untrained voice (which Miss Hewitt had taught him to project) he warbled invitations to Maud to Come into the Garden, to Pretty Jane to meet him in the Evening; to Thora to speak to him; he implored somebody unspecified to Take a Message to his Mother, and a lady called Juanita to Lean upon his Heart. He serenaded Bonnie Mary of Argyll, and reminded Maggie of the days when she and he were young.

And, most remarkable of all, he stayed sober. Mr. Cohen reported his progress to Mr. Abrahams.

'He'th a good boy, a good boy, Morris. But he don't pull 'em in. They geths restless at Belmont'th, especially now there ain't no drinking only in the bar. He ain't enough of a pro and I'm not thure I can recommend him.'

Mr. Abrahams looked pensive. 'Why don't you try out that young daughter of his? If I mistake not, she's got the makings of a comic turn in her, that young lady. Cockney as a penn'orth of whelks, but deuced pretty.'

Mr. Cohen was much struck by this idea, particularly as it implied that he might get a performer cheap. For how could he pay a professional salary to a raw artiste and such a young one? Very subtly he intended to suggest to Clemence that he was doing her an immense favour in rehearsing her in two or three ditties which, if she acquitted herself well, she might be allowed to perform in public with or without her father.

But Clemence, too, could be subtle. When she called upon Mr. Abrahams, at his request, she very soon gathered that her father was not good enough for Belmont's, and that she was expected to fulfil this deficiency at a minimum wage. When she appeared for audition before Mr. Cohen, he was not elated by the sight of her threadbare dress and limp bonnet, or by her demure air, or her quiet Yes Sir and No Sir to his questions. Glancing at his watch, he tersely invited her to sing something, anything. Clemence removed her bonnet, giving Mr. Cohen the benefit of her eyes and her curls. She smiled upon Ernest de Navarro, seated resignedly at the piano.

'Know *The Old Kent Road*, sir?' she asked him.

The pianist indicated gloomily that he did, and went into the prelude.

Clemence stepped back, struck an arms-akimbo attitude,

tilted her chin, and became a cloth-capped, pearly-jacketed coster, as she sang.

'Larst week dahn our alley came a torf,
Nice old geezer, wiv a nasty cough,
Sees my missis, takes 'is topper off
　　In a very gentlemanly way.
"Marm," says 'e, "I've some bad news to tell,
Your rich Uncle Tom in Camberwell
Popped off sudden, which it ain't a sell,
　　Leavin' you 'is little donkey shay."
"Wot cher!" all the neighbours cried,
"Oo're you gonna meet, Bill?
'Ave yer bought the street, Bill?"
Larf! I thought I should 'ave died;
Knocked 'em in the Old Kent Road.'

Whipping her way through the adventures of the donkey and its master, she transformed herself, too swiftly for the pianist to follow her, into the admirer of a talented Spanish lady.

'She sang like a nightingale, twanged a guitar,
Danced the cachuca and smoked a seegar;
　　Oh what a form! Oh what a face!
And she did the fandango all over the place.'

Mr. Cohen held up a fat hand. 'That'll do, girlie.' He turned to Marianne, who was acting as chaperone. 'You got a fine little gal, Ma'am,' he said. 'A bit of experience, and she'll top the bill thome day.'

'What about Dad?' asked Clemence.

What, indeed? Mr. Cohen had almost forgotten his existence. After some discussion it was agreed that Albert and Clemence should try on the early house audience a few duets of a popular kind, such as *The Moon hath Rais'd her Lamp above*. Mr. Cohen gave Clemence an advance on her very small salary to buy suitable clothes. Off she went at her mother's side, alight with happiness, to those alluring

94

shops and stalls in Whitechapel High Road, where smiling Hebrew faces beckoned customers to come and buy their silks and velvets, crepons and serges, cambrics and laces. But when Clemence appeared on the Belmont's stage for the first time it was in the simplest of costumes. She wore a second-hand frock, carefully mended and pressed, of white cotton with a pattern of tiny rosebuds. The sleeves were leg-of-mutton, puffed to the elbow and narrow to the wrist; the bodice was full, in the pouter-pigeon style which was just coming in, and buttoned to the neck, where a little ruffle framed her throat. Her hair was down, flowing on her shoulders; a little hat of yellow straw, with more rosebuds entwining the crown, completed the picture of innocence.

Here, surrounding her, was the wonderful theatre smell, mingled with wafts of beer and onions and oranges. Out there in the semi-dark were faces upon faces, anonymous pale blobs laughing and sighing with her, loving her. Spontaneously she threw open her arms to them, and they shrieked and whistled their approval.

Albert looked on, half glad, half sorry. For all his passion for the theatre he had done nothing worth-while in it, and never would. But his astonishing daughter was a born entertainer, with nerves of iron and the memory of an elephant. Illiterate, she could carry in her head the words of an entire programme, the notes of every tune. He had sired a trouper.

. . . . .

Clemence toured the halls with her father until she was turned fifteen, always wearing the little-girl costume which slew the boys and maddened their grandfathers. She knew her power and rejoiced in it, without becoming vain or precocious. With her open-eyed wondering air she sang words that in another artiste's mouth would have had only one meaning, but in hers seemed so guileless that her audience wondered if they could have heard aright. Ditties such as *Please Light my Little Candle*, *That's what the Soldier said*, and *Oh dear No!* became as nursery rhymes: until you listened carefully to the words.

'My Pussy is so pretty,
　　The prettiest ever yet;
　I wish that you could see her
　　'Cos she's such a little pet . . .'

Absolutely harmless, of course. So was the Omnibus Song.

'I went for a ride on a Homnibus, a Number Seventeen,
But it went all round the 'ouses, all the way to Parsons
　　Green;
The conductor was so friendly, we 'ad a reglar larf,
When I said "Please punch my ticket" 'e answered me
　　"Not 'arf!"
Oh –
Riding on a bus, girls, riding on a bus,
The men are so delightful, they never swear nor cuss,
It's a proper education, when the nights are very dark,
To take a bus from 'Ampstead down to Regent's Park.'

With all this her father could not possibly compete. He
travelled with her, sometimes joining her in a duet, sometimes singing one of the wistful songs which went so well
with his voice and slightly battered handsomeness. Somehow
he had escaped one of the common consequences of heavy
drinking, a bloated reddened face; he looked now like a
blond greying Byron, young in years but old in dissipation.
It was fashionable to look as if one had a Past, in that year
of 1896. A year before Pinero's play, *The Second Mrs.
Tanqueray*, had delighted and shocked London, which
had rocked with amusement at *The Importance of Being
Earnest*, and then turned to hurling abuse at its author,
tried on the hideous charge of sodomy. Havelock Ellis was
working on *Studies in the Psychology of Sex*, Gaugin in
Tahiti painting dusky beauties. Gilbert and Sullivan had
written their last joint opera; the Victorian Age of Innocence was almost over.

　And for Albert Moffat, Fate was lurking in a stage box,
behind a pair of mother-of-pearl lorgnettes.

CHAPTER EIGHT

Miss Lilith de Lisle was enjoying an evening at the Bedford Theatre of Varieties, Camden Town. She had spent a pleasant day shopping in the West End; her opulent bed's gold satin coverlet was almost hidden beneath hatboxes and parcels of all shapes and sizes. Others would follow by messenger. She was particularly pleased with the purchase of an entirely new beauty-cream made from strawberries, guaranteed to preserve the complexion throughout the most rigorous exposure to the elements. (In Miss de Lisle's case, this consisted of the distance between her carriage and the front door of her Gothic-styled house in Park Village.)

She leant her delicately-rouged cheek on a white hand, and gazed complacently at the occupants of the stalls. None, she reflected, was better dressed than she, in her gown of deep gold with an overdress of violet, hiding the daring shoulder-straps which kept up her plunging bodice. Her luxuriant hair was drawn back in the fashionable Grecian knot, and nobody, without close inspection, could have told that its Titian glow came from henna. As for her face, it was as smooth and unlined as a young girl's, though she would never see forty-four again. Around her white neck was a neat carcanet of emeralds set in gold: her really valuable pieces were kept at the bank. Miss de Lisle was a highly successful whore.

She had drifted into the profession on an amateur basis at the age of eighteen, when she discovered her power over men by way of an elderly married colleague of her father's. Frantic for her favours, he had been submitted to a little gentle blackmail accompanied by a long, tantalising wait. When he finally got his wish, it was in return for a financial settlement properly signed and witnessed by a servant.

From the amorous old banker she had progressed steadily upwards, passed on by recommendation, often ending the connection herself when she tired of the gentleman, and moving in higher and higher circles. Her patrons had included a Russian duke, a nouveau riche race horse owner, a very minor connection of the British royal house whom she had banished hurriedly on finding that he was in the early stages of syphilis (anyone can make mistakes), and a Jewish financier whose whim had been to create a mock harem with Lilith, in veils, gauze trousers, and jewels placed at strategic points, as its only occupant.

It had all been interesting, and most profitable. But she was really a little tired of it, ready to turn her attention to some less wearing method of money-making: a directorship on the board of one of the new stores, perhaps. Ponting's and Derry and Toms were said to be good investments. Marriage did not interest her. Her fancy was far too fickle, she knew. She liked to change her lovers as often as her dresses, people said of her. At the moment her heart (or what passed for it) was free. That, she told herself, was why she had gone on that spending spree today. A woman without a lover must compensate herself somehow.

Yes, it was quite time she made another conquest, and of her own choosing this time. Her taste in men was really very good, and she had had to put up with the fat, the ugly, the gauche, the perverted, and the merely plain and boring. This morning she had been horrified to find something very like a wrinkle etched across her brow. Tomorrow there might be another. Why, O why must womanhood be so short-lived, so threatened? She sighed, and turned her attention to the stage.

The crimson curtains had parted for a backcloth of a marble staircase, pillars and statues, the standard one for serious or sentimental songs. At the piano a dark man with a surly expression was playing the prelude. The singer, tall and slender in a black suit, often-pressed, held his music as if it were an offering he was timidly inviting his audience to take. He would, of course, be a tenor, thought Lilith de Lisle, raising her lorgnettes. He was.

'O hoi-ye-ho! ho-ye-ho, who's for the ferry
(The briar's in bud, the sun's going down)
And I'll row ye so quick, and I'll row ye so steady,
And it is but a penny to Twickenham Town.
The ferryman's slim and the ferryman's young,
And he's just a soft twang in the turn of his tongue,
And he's fresh as a pippin, and brown as a berry,
And 'tis but a penny to Twickenham Town.'

A curious sensation stirred in Lilith de Lisle's magnificent bosom. It was as though the vaunted charms of the ferryman were imposing themselves upon the person of the singer, who was certainly slim and comparatively young, and who had a beguiling hint of Cockney in his voice. Beguiling? *Cockney*? She shook her shoulders impatiently. He was somewhere in the next verse.

'O hoi, and oho you may call as you will –
The moon is a-rising on Petersham Hill,
And with love like a rose in the stern of the wherry,
There's danger in crossing to Twickenham Town.'

She leant her arms on the velvet ledge of the box, leaning forward to catch every moment and intonation. Then the song was over, and another followed it, the ever-popular *In the Gloaming*.

Albert was more than a little surprised to receive a note in the dressing-room he shared with three other performers. Nobody had ever sent him a note round before. He read the inscription twice: Mr. Albert Moffat. That was him, undoubtedly. He held the note gingerly away from him as though it might contain a Russian bomb. Then he decided to open it.

'Please attend on me in Box A at the end of the performance.' The signature he found unreadable. Oh well, might be business. He would be there.

'Do come in, Mr. Moffat,' said Miss de Lisle graciously. Albert advanced nervously into the box, a part of the theatre to which he was not used. He felt shabby, seedy, even, in comparison with this finely-dressed lady, some Duchess or whatever. But she was smiling most amiably and patting a chair for him to sit on.

'I enjoyed your songs so much,' she said.

'Did you? Thanks! I thought they didn't go so bad tonight.'

'I wonder if you are free to take me out to supper? I should like to talk to you,' she said pleasantly. Albert's brain reeled. Supper, for a lady like this? However much would it cost? He wouldn't be paid till Friday and even then not as much as would supply *her* with a plate of winkles. Miss de Lisle read his eloquent face.

'Naturally, I shall pay,' she said, 'if you'll allow me. I have a proposition which may interest you.'

The cloud cleared from Albert's brow. Just as he'd thought, this was business. Rich people often hired entertainers for their parties and such; she'd taken a fancy to his style and was going to ask him to sing at her next At Home. He wondered if old Navarro would be cut in on the deal, and rather hoped not.

'Thanks very much – er – Miss. It'll be a pleasure.'

She rose, regally handing him her cloak, with its edging of rich fur. As he put it round her shoulders she took no advantage of their proximity; there was plenty of time.

At the stage-door, where her carriage waited, he excused himself and went back inside. She saw him talking to a young girl, a pretty dark creature who kissed him warmly in parting. A stab of jealousy startled her, but his words were reassuring as he settled himself at her side.

'Just had to tell my girl to go on home by herself.'

'Your daughter?'

'That's it. My eldest. We do a double singing act, Clem and me.'

'You have other children, then?'

'Yes, two more. Be another one by Christmas.' His smile was half-frank, half-shy. She found it delightful. 'The Café Royal,' she told the driver; and with a flick of the whip the carriage was on its way.

Never, in his wildest dreams, had Albert seen anything so like the poor man's Paradise as the Café Royal. The glittering chandeliers, the furnishings, the crimson and the gilt, the scurrying waiters and rich diners, the casual air of the place, suggesting that nobody would bother to go home till morning all combined to make him feel as if he had unexpectedly died. But his senses told him it was real. Rich, savoury food-smells roused his hunger, the icy sweetness of champagne from a bottle in a silver pail woke him like a splash from a fountain; the heady perfume of Prince of Wales' Bouquet wafting from his hostess's white shoulders and freely displayed bosom had yet another effect. Somehow, though the meal in the Café Royal's best private room had begun most decorously, towards the end of it his hand was upon Miss de Lisle's silken knee and his mouth was exploring one lovely shoulder from which the golden strap had slipped away.

'Yes,' he said thickly. 'Yes, yes, darling.'

。　　　　　ā　　　　　。　　　　　・　　　　　ꝯ

Marianne was a little peevish at being wakened in the small hours of the morning by her husband's ostentatiously quiet return. She was beginning an inquisition, but he refused to talk. ' 'Sallright. Tell you in the morning,' he said, and in a moment was asleep.

When his explanation was given, Marianne and Clemence received it open-mouthed. '*Manservant*? to a *lady*? But you've never been in service!'

'Well, not manservant exactly,' Albert said, shifting with the unease of one who has not told many downright whopping lies in all his life. 'More like general duties. Can't explain, really' (which was only too true). 'But it's a proper soft job, all found, lots of perks.'

Marianne's brows were still knotted. 'I still don't understand why she picked *you*.'

'Probably fancies him,' said Clemence. '*I* would,' and she sent her father a knowing wink. 'Anyway, don't let's grumble, if it's going to pay like Dad says – better money

101

than he'd get doing the circuits if he was at it ten years.'

'That's it, Clem,' Albert put in. 'With what I bring home at weekend there'll be better living for all of us – no need for you to go traipsing about for your old sewing jobs, now you're getting . . .' his eyes glanced over her figure, clumsy already at five months.

'Can Sophy have a dolly?' asked his younger daughter, who missed nothing.

'Yes, Sophy can have a dolly, with open-and-shut eyes,' said Albert recklessly, 'and poor old Charlie shall go to Margate and get some sea air into his lungs.' He ruffled his son's pale hair, happy that what he was saying now was at least true. ' 'Course, I shan't be able to go round with you now, Clem. You'll need a chaperone.'

'Amy,' said Clemence promptly. Amy was Bella's second daughter, a year older than Clemence but her devoted slave. 'Amy'll go anywhere with me, and she can bring her knitting. Knit a donkey's hind leg off, she would.'

'Then it's settled,' said Albert, considerably relieved. 'And I'll be home every Friday, Marianne, I promise you. Miss de Lisle particularly said I was to have weekends, being a family man.'

'That's good of her.' More evenings alone, thought Marianne; more evenings with the comforting bottle by her side, the bottle which was her refuge from worries about Charlie's health and Sophy's growing out of her clothes, Albert's unfaithfulness and the possibility of Clemence being ruined by gentlemen. And, worst of all, the worry that she was losing her looks, that Albert didn't love her any more.

Drink had been useless. It had only made her ugly and bad-tempered, so that in the morning she hated herself for what she had done and said, hated the sickly sweet smell of the cup that had held four penn'orth of gin. Now she had something much, much better. She glanced affectionately towards the pot-cupboard by the bed, where she kept the morphine bottle.

It was a day for celebration in Black Lion Court when Albert came home with his first wages. He looked sleek and pleased with himself after a week of good eating and the nameless comforts and joys of Miss de Lisle's five-foot bed. She had actually bought him a new jacket, pearl-grey, very smart; wasn't it kind of her? Full of love for mankind, Albert gave Marianne the warmest embrace for years, after which she hurried to pin her best lace jabot on to her blouse and dab on some scent from the bottle of Chypre Albert had given her so long ago that it was only the ghost of its former self.

Of course the money had to be counted out: two whole sovereigns! Sophy was sent upstairs to call Bella to come down and see. 'A tea-party!' said that lady, having feasted her eyes on these riches. 'We ain't 'ad one since Polly's wedding.' Clemence and Albert were to go out and fetch a pound of Choice Blend, a loaf and some butterine ('not stale, mind'), some shrimps and watercress and Golden Syrup and a sticky iced cake each for the children.

'Which it does me good to see 'em,' said Bella, 'being as mine's grown and gone. Sam's orf work with 'is rheumatics, so 'e can be toaster.'

Sam was only too pleased to occupy a warm place by the fire, toasting fork in hand, adding crisp slice after crisp slice to the pile Bella was butterine-ing. 'Can't Inkerman come?' pleaded Sophy.

'Don't be silly!' Charlie told her with scorn. 'He couldn't manage the stairs.'

'Inkerman shall 'ave 'is share, Charlie,' Sam promised. 'Likes a bit o' cress, does the old chap.' Resolutely he banished the thought, so often with him now, of the time when Inkerman, an old chap indeed, would no more be fit to draw the cab. There was only one end for an old cab-horse; he couldn't bear to contemplate it. Clemence, with her uncanny intuition, read his thoughts.

'I been thinking, Mr. Clickett, Dad's lady might own some place in the country, where she could farm Inkerman out when he can't work no more.'

Sam brightened instantly. 'So she might. What abaht puttin' the word on 'er, Albert?'

Albert admitted that Miss de Lisle had mentioned a small house she had, somewhere convenient for hunting, her favourite outdoor sport. Perhaps Charlie could go there for a holiday, he thought. He had told Miss de Lisle about Charlie, and what the doctor said, and she had smiled and seemed to listen, though he somehow gathered that she was not particularly fond of children. He had been slightly shocked by a story she had told him about the French tart who had had a road-sign put up above her bedroom door: 'Prenez-garde aux enfants.'

They had eaten all the food except for Inkerman's share, and drunk two potsful of the Choice Blend. The firelight was flickering cheerfully on the flushed faces in the crowded room; outside the lamplighter's star-tipped wand brought lamp after lamp alive in the November dusk.

'Clem, read the teacups for us,' said Bella.

'Not now, I've got a lazy bone.'

'Oh, go on! Tell your Dad's fortune.'

Clemence shrugged, and reached for Albert's cup. 'All right, but I'm not in the mood.' She turned the cup this way and that, studied the tea-leaves that clung to its sides. 'I told you, I can't see nothing.'

'Well, your Mum's, then. Tell 'er what the next little 'un's goin' to be.'

Marianne handed her cup to Clemence, who took it reluctantly. What she saw in it made her freeze for a moment; then she said, 'It's all blurred and silly. I told you so. Come on, Amy, if you want us to get to the Phil for first house. It's getting foggy.'

Amy was not anxious to leave the warm fire for a chilly walk to the Philharmonic at Islington, but Clemence's word was law. Obediently she uncurled herself, and went to get ready. Albert, too, said he must go. Miss de Lisle had kindly given him the afternoon off, but he was wanted for a supper party she was giving. (He omitted to mention that the party would consist of himself and Lady Lilith, as she liked to be called after some story-book character or other, and another couple.) Marianne, disappointed, was inclined to sulk, but was brought round by Sophy, who fortuitously choked on a crumb of cake and had to be restored with vigorous back slappings.

Albert kissed the children and Marianne, adding a consolatory pat on the bottom. 'Don't I get no kiss?' Bella asked plaintively. He took her face in his hands (it was still a handsome face) and gave her a hearty kiss. Clemence came back, cloaked and bonneted.

'Good night, Dad,' she said. 'Wish we were going the same way.'

'Wish we were. Can't be helped. Got your music?'

They walked down the bare staircase together, Amy behind them. At the street door Albert kissed Clemence, and as they parted to go their separate ways he turned and raised his hat gallantly to the two girls. For a moment they saw him in the yellow light from the lamp at the corner, dapper and smiling. Then the fog swallowed him, and he was gone.

.   .   .   .   .

He was lucky enough to board an omnibus that would take him within ten minutes' walk or so of Park Village. Getting off by the church at the corner of the Euston Road and Albany Street, he wrapped his scarf round his mouth, as wise Londoners did on such a night of yellow murk, and set off at a brisk pace up Albany Street. Past the sedate houses of Colosseum Terrace, he reached the mews and the lights of the little Chester Arms. They beckoned warmly; he obeyed, and went in.

The winter speciality of the Chester Arms was rum punch, served from an aromatic steaming bowl. Albert partook gratefully of two glasses of it before moving on, lighter of foot and euphoric of soul. Further up the street was the Cumberland, where he thought he might refuel for the rest of the journey. There was no punch, but black Navy rum and hot water made an adequate substitute. When he came out, the fog seemed thicker; or perhaps it was his eyes. The backs of the noble Nash houses facing Regent's Park were no longer faint ghosts – they had vanished altogether. Only the exotic cries of birds and animals from the Zoological Gardens told him where he was. Park Village, and the delights of the Gothic house and its mistress – *his* mistress! – lay only round the corner. But he had pleasant memories of the York and Albany, a particularly cheerful hostelry round in Park Street. Lady Lilith wouldn't object to a man being slightly whistled, cut, one over the eight. Not she!

'Save a little bit off the top for me, for me,' he sang, 'Just a little bit off the top for me . . .'

There was an old pal in the York and Albany, that very stage-door keeper from the Park Street theatre who had told Albert to try the East End theatres. Their reunion was joyous, for Sidney, too, had been fortifying himself against the fog. Over steaming glasses, Albert, with tears of sentiment in his eyes, confided in his friend.

''Stonishing piece of luck ever had. Beautiful woman – fi' woman. Wife's a fi' woman too. Mean t' do the bess I can for her and the kids. Never been much good to 'em, Sid o' man. Weak. Weak.' He drew a melancholy path along the counter with his wet glass. 'Marianne, thass my wife, she was a lovely girl. But shouldn' married. Too young. Both too young. No money. Fam'ly cut me off with a shilling. Not even a shilling, come to think. Have 'nother.'

Both their glasses were speedily refilled.

'All change now,' continued Albert. 'All change, like conduc – con-duc-tor says.' He laughed uproariously. 'Plenty of the stuff now. All for making love to fi' woman. Money for jam!'

Sidney queried the appropriateness of the latter noun, to the immense amusement of both.

'Norramoral,' Albert pronounced solemnly. 'Not – immoral. Lil – Lilith's gorra heart of gold. Glad help my poor fam'ly. Horse, even poor old horse . . .' He lost his train of thought. The striking of the bar clock recalled to Sidney's mind that he was due at the theatre and, bidding Albert a friendly good-night, he left.

Albert finished his drink and followed him, roseate with good-fellowship and dreams. The dank foggy air hit him in the face like a slap from a giant's cold hand. Uncertain which way he should be facing, he moved forward to the pavement's edge, reeled as two bright lights came at him out of the fog, and fell beneath the wheels of an omnibus bound for St. John's Wood.

．　　．　　．　　．　　．

It was eight o'clock before Lilith became at all worried about her cavalier. The thick fog explained his lateness; her guests were late as well. She dressed slowly and carefully in a new claret-coloured silk from Harrod's, with a Medici collar that framed her head in points of gold lace. She drove her maid to the point of desperation by her insistence on a new styling of her hair to fit the collar. ('Pernickety bitch!' hissed the maid to the cook in the kitchen. 'Dressed up like a dog's dinner for the new feller, and him no better than you and me, I reckon!')

Eight-fifteen. Lilith descended to the drawing-room and allowed herself a small sherry, against her usual custom. The Prince of Wales might flourish on the cocktail habit, but it had an unpleasant effect on the female complexion.

At a quarter to nine her guests arrived; a lady in circumstances similar to hers, and a strapping Guards officer a good deal younger. They were cold and cross after a tedious journey from Bayswater. Lilith decided that it would be wise to serve dinner at once if anything of the evening were to be salvaged. In fact, Cook had prepared a delicious ragout which, with a '69 Burgundy, completely restored the guests' good temper; Lilith gracefully concealed her own annoyance and disappointment, resolving to give Master Albert Moffat a piece of her mind when he came to apologise next morning.

．　　．　　．　　．　　．

But he didn't come. It was a police constable who rang her bell next day. She was in the morning-room, fuming with temper, a tray of coffee and biscuits at her side. Confound Albert, she thought, he *would* choose to slink back before she had even tasted the coffee just poured. As the door opened she began to say, 'So you've condescended –' Then she saw the uniform.

'Miss de Lisle?'

'Yes.' Her tone was wary. There were passages in her life which, if brought to light, might well have interested the police.

'I'm afraid I may have bad news for you, miss. This visiting-card of yours was found in the pocket of a man –'

'Picked up drunk in the street, I suppose you're going to say! Well, you needn't ask me to bail him out, or whatever the proper thing is, because I shall do no such thing.'

'He was picked up in the street, miss, but dead, not drunk. Run over in the fog, it's thought, just up the road, in Park Street. There were papers on him to indicate that his name was Albert Moffat, but the only address we could find was yours.' He held out a gilt-edged card with a dark stain across it which he didn't bother to conceal. She looked at it impassively.

'I see,' she said. 'That explains it.'

'You did know this man, then, miss?'

'He was an employee of mine, engaged only a week ago.'

The policeman produced a notebook. 'Perhaps you'd be kind enough to give me the address of any relatives.'

'Relatives? I've no idea, I'm sure. I believe he had a family in the East End somewhere.'

'Ah,' said the policeman thoughtfully. 'Can you possibly think of any connection that'd help to find them – a name, something he might have mentioned?' Lilith frowned. This person was evidently going to be troublesome. She adjusted a tendril of hair.

'I suppose you could try the Bedford Theatre. I believe he performed there sometimes.'

'The Bedford.' He was writing it down. 'In that case, I'll

get along there now. Thank you, miss. You'll be informed, of course, when the relatives are found – naturally you'll want to get in touch with them. Good day.'

She watched him go, heard the front door shut after him. Get in touch with relatives, indeed, and find herself saddled with a lot of yowling women and children, all expecting charity! Not bloody likely.

Her beautiful face changed from scorn to melancholy. How sad. So handsome – in a common way– and so amusing in bed. Ah well. She picked up the morning paper and began to scan the entertainment columns, sipping her neglected coffee.

It had gone cold, and she poured it away.

CHAPTER NINE

The news reached Black Lion Yard early that evening. All day Clemence had paced restlessly about, running to the window whenever anyone entered from the street – which was very often. 'Sit still, Clem, won't you, or learn a song or something,' her mother said, irritated. 'It makes me jumpy to look at you. Dad'll be home sometime.'

· 'He *said* after breakfast,' Clemence repeated. 'He said his lady was going up West and he wouldn't be wanted.'

'Well, who knows what may have happened to change his mind?'

Clemence shrugged unhappily. 'Anything, I s'pose. Come on, you two, let's get out. I'm sick of sitting here smelling yesterday's kippers.'

'You're never taking Charlie out on a day like this? It's coming up foggy again, he'll get one of his attacks!'

'Not if I wrap him up he won't. And Sophy, you can just put those boots on again. No, I know they ain't your best, but they're thicker than what you've got on.' Amid shrieks and complaints, the children were dressed and taken firmly out into the chilly afternoon on their usual Saturday promenade to the Great Synagogue, to see the rich Jewish gentlemen and their fine ladies coming and going, and to walk round the Portuguese Jews' burying-ground in Mile End Road, where Charlie enjoyed spelling out the exotic names. 'Look, Clem, it says here BENJAMIN D'ISRAELI,' he said. 'That's the man we've learnt about at school.' (But his teacher had omitted to tell him that the grave so near to the school was that of the statesman's grandfather.) Clemence gave Charlie's arm a sharp tug.

'Well, well, we *are* fine scholars, aren't we. Now come on, we'll all catch our death.'

'Clem's jealous 'cause Charlie and me can read,' jeered Sophy, skipping. 'Clem's jealous, jealous, jealous!' This was only too true, and gall to Clemence's ambitious soul. 'Shut up!' she snapped, and walked quickly and haughtily on ahead. Near the gates she paused and whipped round, holding out her arms with a smile. 'There! I'm sorry. I'm a cross-tempered cat today, lovies.' They all linked arms and walked amicably home, Charlie stealing a glance of wistful enquiry into his sister's face. He too missed his father, and worried. Outside the London Hospital they saw a muffin-man, summoning with his cheerful cry and his bell those within doors to buy some comfort for a winter's dusk. Clemence bought some.

Marianne had the kettle on the hob; a liberal helping of the Choice Blend tea was waiting in the warmed pot, and the muffins cooked sweetly. As they ate, Marianne looked round the room speculatively.

'We might be getting something better than this to live in, one day,' she said. 'Little place – oh, I don't know – somewhere with a bit of garden.' She lifted from the mantelpiece the cherub-figure with the dangling hearts, intact and brightly smiling through all these years. 'I'll always remember when your Dad gave me this. It was a beautiful day, we were going on the train . . .'

A knock sounded on the street door, that door on which people did not usually knock. To Clemence it was as though the clock stopped, and her heart, and time. She took the figurine from her mother's hand, replaced it on the mantelpiece, and went out on the landing.

'Who d'you want?' she called.

'Name of Moffat.'

'Up here.'

Sturdy boots climbed the stairs, and a slightly breathless policeman stood at the door, wishing earnestly that he were anywhere else. Even with the amazing new telephone instrument, so enterprisingly installed by his chiefs, the discovery of the address of Albert Moffat had taken hours, and when he had arrived in early for the evening shift he had found himself posted for a disagreeable duty.

'I'm very sorry to have to tell you, ma'am . . .'

111

Sophy burst into tears, and would not be comforted. Charlie went greenish-pale, and began to choke and gasp for air; the asthmatic's reaction to shock. Mechanically, Clemence soaked a cloth in the hot water from the kettle, and treated his attack as she always did, meanwhile saying 'Yes, sir,' and 'No, sir' to the constable's remarks. Marianne sat motionless and silent, like a woman in a trance. He was saying something about identifying the body.

'Yes, sir, I'll do it. Mum, you see, she's not able . . .'

The policeman compassionately glanced at the swollen figure of the widow. 'I see, yes. Then if you'd come along to the station in the morning, miss, you'll be taken to the – to the mortuary.'

Marianne came to life. 'You mean there might be a mistake? It mightn't be him?'

'I'm afraid I can't promise that, ma'am. From the description given at the theatre it seemed pretty clear . . .'

'Yes.' She relapsed.

As he was leaving, Clemence followed him out and shut the door.

'Will you do something to help me, please, sir?'

'Anything, love.' He was a fatherly man, and would have done anything in his power to have cured the grief in the blue eyes which would not cry before the family.

'This telephone, that you can talk to Camden Town on. Could you – would you talk to them at the Bedford Theatre? I've seen one on the manager's office wall. Tell them I won't be on tonight, and – and why?'

'I can't do it myself, my dear, but I'll see it's done.'

Those happy souls who, like sundials, prefer to register only the shining hours, do not hoard and count over such times in their lives as the days that followed in Clemence's. She lived through them and carried the weight of them, for she was the strongest. It fell to her to endure the journey to the mortuary, where something still and cold lay under a covering on a slab. In that same mortuary, and on that same slab, one of the Ripper's mutilated victims had lain.

Yes, it was her father. At least, it looked like him, but different. No, thank you, she wouldn't like a drink. Yes, she could get home all right. Her mother was all right, a neighbour was with her and the children. Thank you for the shillings from Dad's pocket, very kind of you. About the funeral, she didn't know, but she thought the neighbour, Mrs. Clickett, would.

Of course Bella did. With swift authority she took the grim arrangements over, 'used as I am to lyin's-in and layin's-out, my dear,' as she realistically remarked. Polly and her husband were alerted, and Joe drove over from Peckham in his donkey-cart to take Sophy back to Polly's embrace and the consolation of Polly's new baby, while at home Clemence nursed Charlie through what promised to be a serious attack, complicated by his ceaseless tears.

'Thank Gawd 'e *is* ill,' Bella said. 'Keeps you from goin' broody, Clem, not that you would. It's 'er I worry abaht, sittin' there like a stone idol. T'ain't natural not to cry.' For Marianne had sat all day, half-smiling, in a dream, it seemed, staring in front of her, hardly moving or speaking. She accepted a cup of tea, drank half, then seemed to forget it. Her eyes roved languidly over Clemence, Charlie in his bed, the changing light from the window, the smoke-darkened ceiling and peeling wallpaper. Once she laid her hands over the mound that was her unborn child, and said with the same vague smile 'He isn't kicking any more. Perhaps he's dead, too.'

'It's no use,' Bella whispered to Clemence. 'She's got to be shocked aht of it. Sometimes you've to be cruel to be kind.' Drawing a stool up by Marianne's chair, she took her hand.

'Listen to me, my duckie, and don't pretend you're deaf, 'cause Bella knows better. You've lorst your 'usband, you know. 'E's gone and 'e won't come back. Now let's talk abaht it. We liked your Albert, Sam and me. Made for better things, 'e was, so clever and with that lovely voice of 'is. Won't you cry for 'im a bit, my dear?'

Marianne turned her head slowly and looked at Bella for

113

the first time. 'It was another woman,' she said. 'He went to another woman. I could smell her scent on his jacket.'

Hers was something stranger than grief; the defeat of a woman's pride, beyond rescue now that Death, the last rival, had taken her man. Before there had been hope, and now there was none.

Bella had gone upstairs, Charlie was uneasily asleep after a heavy dose of the calmative medicine the doctor had left for him. Clemence had seen her mother undress, and take down her waist-length hair. Now she sat by the fire, brushing it with long, slow strokes. Clemence went to her.

'Would you like me to sleep with you, Mum?'

'No, dear. I'm all right.' With the first warmth she had shown that day she drew Clemence's face down, and kissed her. 'Good girl,' she said. Clemence went back to her own bed. She thought she would never sleep after such a day, but exhaustion overcame her as soon as her head touched the pillow. She began to drift, drift into blessed oblivion, with a dim, fading consciousness of the slow, crackling sound of the hairbrush, and of a louder crackling as though the fire were burning brighter than it had been. Then sleep came and set her free.

It was morning when she woke to the rumble of carts and rattle of bottles from the pub, and all the noises of a street astir. Charlie was sleeping peacefully, the blueness gone from his face, she was thankful to see. She tiptoed over to the bed where her mother lay quiet. Usually she snuggled beneath the bedclothes, but this morning her head was uncovered, the hair spread loose on the pillow, not plaited as usual. Her eyes were closed and she was smiling, but Clemence knew before she touched the cold hand under the cold cheek that she was looking upon death for the second time.

In the grate, among the ashes, lay the burnt fragments of a doll's bright-patterned dress, and an unconsumed black head from which the sawdust had trickled.

On the pot-cupboard by the bed was a little brown bottle with a chemist's label, quite empty.

'That's what I saw in her teacup,' Clemence said aloud to the quiet room. 'No future. Nothing.'

     ▪   •   ▪   •   •

Everybody was so kind. Not just Bella, who organised a whip-round among the tenants to help with the money for the double burial, and who was generally a pillar of strength; or Sam, sacrificing half a day's fares so that Sophy and Charlie should ride with him behind the slow-pacing Inkerman, down to the docks to see the ships loading and unloading, on the day of the funeral. There was the cross old man from upstairs whom they'd always regarded as a sort of hermit who hated everybody; now he came down with pathetic offerings of what he considered suitable for the consolation of children: a boxful of colourful cut-outs to stick on a screen, an old toy coach made of tin. The people from the Black Lion came to the funeral, and all sorts of theatre folk sent flowers and wreaths.

Clemence wished they wouldn't. It made everything so much worse. She was glad that there was no question of going into black, like the rich did. Even among the poorest in Whitechapel there were those who would have scrounged and even stolen to get mourning garments for the glorification of Death, but Clemence said: 'Even if we was well off Mum and Dad wouldn't want us going round like a lot of old crows,' and she went proudly in her usual clothes, which were sombre and shabby enough to acquit her on any charge of light-mindedness.

Now they were orphans. The dead were dead, but the living must live; the question was, how?

The only person Clemence trusted to give her sensible advice was Mr. Abrahams, who had helped her before. Ever courteous and kind, he received her as if she had been a visiting Rothschild, and listened to her tale with as much patience as a man who had nothing to occupy him for the next few hours. At its conclusion his eyebrows rose.

'But surely you can get work in the theatre? You have had some success already, your name is beginning to be known. Why throw away connections you have already made?'

She shook her head stubbornly. 'I know all that, sir, and it's no good, not with my two to keep. Now Dad's gone I won't get the work I did when we'd our double act. And I'm not what you might call experienced. I'm a bit of a natural, ain't I?' Her old merry smile shone out. 'Get the bird once, and you might as well move into the nest.'

Mr. Abrahams sighed. It was all too true. A mere child like this, not sixteen, would be taking a mammoth risk in embarking alone on the treacherous sea of entertainment, where a face suddenly spoilt by smallpox or a voice unluckily hoarse might lose her a living; and where her body would be regarded as the normal payment for favours received from managements and influential artistes.

'What else can you do?' he asked.

'I can sew, sir. Anything at all. Make me own clothes, do embroidery, plain sewing, all the lot. My Mum learnt it from the nuns and taught me.'

After a short struggle, Mr. Abrahams made up his mind. 'I have a brother who is a tailor. He has an establishment where women and girls make garments for sale to shops – not to individual orders, you understand.'

Clemence nodded. 'Mum only did customer work.'

'I see very little of my brother.' Mr. Abrahams' expression suggested that this caused him no sorrow. 'He is reasonably prosperous, and I imagine his workpeople are no worse off than – are paid as well as most. It's not good pay, you understand,' he waved his hands expressively. 'I would not like to deceive you, Miss Moffat. All I know is that it is steady work and would permit you to live at home, so that you could continue to look after your young sister and brother.' He paused, studying the pretty downcast head, the face meant for laughter, the body for love and pretty clothes. Once again he tried to impress her with the advice conscience or instinct were whispering in his ear.

'I will be frank with you, Miss Moffat. You are a sensible young woman and I speak to you as one. There is a rift in our family. I and my house are Sephardic Jews, faithful to our belief as well as to our race. We are Orthodox. You understand?'

'Yes, sir.' Clemence had seen the rooms of such families, though poorer ones than his, lit on Friday night with the seven-branched candlestick, while the ritual food was served and prayers were said. It was all very interesting and pretty.

'My brother has seceded from the Faith.' He saw her puzzlement. 'He has ceased to attend our synagogue and no longer lives by our rites. It has caused a great breach between us. My wife and I do not visit him, nor he us. There is no quarrel; it is a matter of religion, you understand.'

Clemence could hardly have said she did, brought up in an atmosphere of haphazard churchgoing, but she made an intelligent face and imagined Mr. Abrahams and Mrs. Abrahams and all the young Abrahamses round the white-spread table eating gefilte fish and kosher butter and other things seen on Whitechapel stalls. It was a pleasant escape from remembering what had happened at home; she hardly heard what else Mr. Abrahams was saying about his brother, but came to herself when he handed her a note in an addressed envelope. Her eyelids drooped on suddenly flushed cheeks.

'If you please – could you read it me, sir.'

Kindly he said 'My writing is bad, I know' (it was a particularly elegant copperplate), and read the address, which was in Arbour Street, off Commercial Road. Then he said:

'Before you go to see my brother, will you not think again? Believe me, I would do my utmost to help you to earn a living in the theatre.'

'Thank you, sir. But I'll have a go at this first.'

Sadly he watched her out of sight. He would not like to have seen a good Jewish girl, a daughter of his, seek employment from Isaac Abrahams.

Arbour Street, like so many poetically christened London thoroughfares, belied its name. If there had ever been an arbour in or near it, its leaves had withered long ago. It was surrounded by grimy buildings, lodgings let to sailors, slop-

117

shops kept by the crimps who fitted out Jack ashore at an extortionate price, rooms which housed the women who lived off Jack's money. Black, brown and yellow faces were commoner here than white ones; no night passed without a fight of some sort, knife or fists. Second-hand clothes filled the air with their peculiar stench; in dirty windows here and there hung a miserable parrot, left as a pledge by a Jack with empty pockets, swearing monotonously to itself. As Clemence walked down Arbour Street her cloak was pulled by a leering man lounging in a doorway, and a suggestion made which brought flames to her cheeks. She hurried to the street number she had memorised, No. 17.

If her heart had sunk before it plummeted into her boots as she pushed open the door, once painted with yellowish varnish but now almost stripped. A fascia over the window said I. ABRAHAMS MASTER TAILOR, only partly obscuring the painted-out sign of a long-departed butcher, of whose habitation the only other evidence was a row of hooks under a small projecting canopy.

The narrow lobby led straight to a flight of stairs whose condition suggested that Mr. Abrahams's domestic staff didn't include a charlady. 'Bloomin' Grand Staircase, Buckingham Palace, I don't think,' Clemence said to herself, 'Buck up, might be a pleasant surprise inside.' She knocked firmly on the door on the left. There was no reply. After a further salvo of knocks a peevish voice called 'Come in, can't yer?' She obeyed.

What had been the butcher's shop was an office, judging by a grey tin filing-cabinet, a deal table strewn with papers, and a desk at which a pale spotty boy was sitting, licking an envelope. They eyed each other with mutual distaste.

'Wotcher want?' he enquired, his eyes roving insultingly over her figure, as the departed butcher may have viewed a Smithfield carcass.

'I want Mr. Abrahams, that's who I want,' Clemence retorted. 'And in case you should be so kind as to ask why, I've got a letter from his brother, Mr Morris Abrahams, of the Pavilion Theatre.'

'Ho, 'ave yer,' mocked the youth. 'Well, Yer Bloody Ladyship, *hif* yer can possibly spare a minute of yer vallible time, I'll see if 'e's at 'ome to visitors.' While Clemence tapped her foot with temper, he opened another door and shouted 'Young woman for yer' after which he resumed his writing. Clemence saw that he was making out bills.

The person who responded to his summons was a tall, balding, black-suited man who might have been sixty or thereabouts. Clemence, who had vaguely expected a twin of her Mr. Abrahams, was cast down to see that only a mother's eye could have detected any resemblance between them. In place of Morris's opulent good looks, Isaac's appearance was bilious and seedy. His eyes were drooping and baggy, his lips drooped similarly, with a cruel cast to them. He didn't even look particularly Jewish, she thought; at the most, he might have been a failed auditionee for Shylock in a fourth-rate touring company. His suit was of good cloth, but on him might as well have been of the same material as Inkerman's horse blanket. Clemence took an instant violent dislike to him. But she had come on business, and business was what mattered, with a family to keep.

'Well?' he said.

Clemence produced his brother's note and handed it over. 'Your brother Mr. Morris sent this to recommend me,' she said. Isaac read it without visible pleasure, then eyed her disparagingly.

'So you want work?'

'Wouldn't be here else, would I?' She sensed that politeness would be wasted upon Isaac.

'That's enough of your lip!'

'I'm not staying to be spoken to like that,' she told him. 'I may want work but I don't want it that bad.' As she turned on her heel he called her back.

'Not so fast. No need to take offence. I can do with another girl here, yes. You can sew, my brother says.'

'I am an expert needlewoman,' said Clemence with pride. 'Anything from handkerchieves to ladies' robes and mantles.' Isaac sneered.

119

'You won't be asked to make robes and mantles here, young woman. Shirts and trousers, that's what I supply, to the trade only. *And* I pay by quantity. Quality I take for granted. Here's my rates, take 'em or leave 'em.' He handed her a dirty card. She looked at it blankly, seeing only meaningless marks and figures. In her mind a battle raged: should she admit her illiteracy and be mocked, as these two would be sure to mock her, or pretend she could read? Flustered, she stared at the writing. Pride conquered.

'That's all right,' she said airily. Isaac snatched the card back from her. To the clerk he said 'Put her down to start tomorrow, Jody.'

'Can't I start today?' she asked eagerly.

'You've got cottons to buy, haven't you?' snapped Isaac. 'Provide your own cottons here, that's our rule. You'll want white, grey and black, and strong twine, mind.'

When she turned up next morning with the cotton-reels which had cost her all the money she had after paying her own share of the burial money and buying food for the children, she had to summon up all her courage to enter. Jody was sitting in the office, as before, cleaning his nails with a paper-knife. When Clemence asked where she was to go he jerked his thumb in the direction of the stairs, making no response to her thanks. She could feel him staring after her as she went out. Near the top of the stairs she turned, to see him standing in the lobby looking up at her and grinning. She realised that she'd been holding her skirts high to keep them from trailing on the filthy treads, thus giving him an uninterrupted view of her legs. Angrily she dropped them and marched into the room at the top from which she could hear a murmur of voices.

It was a moderate-sized square room, once a bedchamber. The iron fireplace had been blocked up; there was no other form of heating. The window was uncurtained – the proprietor found this cheaper than providing more lighting in addition to the one gas wall-bracket. In one corner a woman with her back to the door was working a sewing-machine, its monotonous treadle-noise mingling with the murmuring conversation of the women and girls who sat about on the floor, each with a piece of material on which she was working. Some of the sempstresses were half-ragged, others poorly dressed but with some sort of neatness about their dress and hair. They were all sitting cross-legged, some on cushions formed by their own coats folded twice. (In *Punch* a savage caricature had appeared, a drawing of cross-legged skeletons stitching away, watched by a fat and self-satisfied overseer.)

Clemence had lived in a poor home, among poor people, but their poverty had been decent. In the streets she had seen plenty who lived among filth – some who were literally starving – and had smelt the stench of human decay. But a child's imagination is not awake to unseen suffering; until she entered the sewing-room Clemence had not fully comprehended her world.

Her world! Was it to be this? In a moment of time, standing in the doorway, inspected by eyes inquisitive, envious, sullen or indifferent, she regretted bitterly that she had not begged Morris Abrahams to get her into anything but this. A menial job in the theatre, what bliss it would be, in comparison! But she would not have been Clemence if she had flinched and run away. 'Here you are, and you might as well make the best of it, you silly fool,' she said to herself; and aloud she said: 'Good morning.'

One of the women spoke, the same gracious words with which Jody had greeted her yesterday.

'Wotcher want?'

'I've come to work here,' Clemence said, smiling artificially.

'Vy doncher go and 'ang yerself instead? Be a bloody sight quicker.'

Clemence, ignoring this pleasantry, enquired what she was to do. The woman tossed over a garment from the top of a pile, hitting Clemence in the face with it. 'Get on wiv those trahsers,' she said without apology.

'What am I to do with them?' Clemence asked. There was a general snigger. 'Wot the workus beadle did with the Christmas pudden, if yer like,' said the spokeswoman, 'but they wants button'olin'.'

Clemence examined them, her hesitation causing another ripple of mirth. 'Guess all she knows about trahsers is wot goes in 'em,' said the woman to the others. 'Aincher never seen fly-buttons before, ducky?'

Clemence felt herself going fiery red. She set her lips, without answering, and prepared to start work. The only place in the room with any degree of light was the area in front of the window, already crowded. She looked towards it, and was told roughly: 'T'other side, you! New gals over there.'

Over there on the opposite side of the room was practically in darkness. Clemence went over to it, took off her hat, keeping her coat on for warmth, and sat down on the floor. A packet of needles was thrown to her, and the woman told her that each pair of scissors was shared by two women. 'Kind of 'Is Nibs, ain't it. A wonder 'e don't expect us to use our teeth.' As the woman had very few of the latter, Clemence thought that on the whole this was a good thing. Politely she asked the thin dark girl next to her for the use of the scissors, and smiled when they were handed to her. She straightened her back so as to be as comfortable as possible, and began to sew.

Fragments of tunes came into her mind, ridiculously inappropriate, playing over and over again like music from a barrel-organ. Without intent she began to hum, then to sing softly, below the noise of the machine and the chatter.

'Don't make a noise, or else you'll wake the baby,
Don't make a noise, or else you'll wake the child,
Don't make a noise or you'll disturb the infant,
I feel so awf'lly, awf'lly jolly I think I shall go wild.'

A wry grin appeared on the dark girl's face.
'You won't feel jolly for long,' she said.
'All the more reason to chirp a bit while I feel like it,'

122

Clemence returned. She threw a sly glance at her neighbours and saw that they were listening as she began again.

'My old man is a very clever chap, 'e's an artist in the
    Royal Academy.
He paints pictures from mornin' till night –
Paints 'em with 'is left hand, paints 'em with 'is right –
All 'is pictures, take a tip from me, are very very Eve
    and Adamy,
And I'm the model who poses for him in the garden all
    day long.
Ooh –
It's all right in the summertime,
In the summertime, it's lovely –
My old man sits paintin' 'ard
While I'm posing in the old back yard.
But oh, oh, in the wintertime,
It's another tale, you know;
With very few clothes
And a little red nose,
And the stormy winds do blow.'

'Come on, girls! What about a bit of a chorus?' Tentatively, one or two voices joined thinly as she began the verse again. Then more were added, until ten or twelve of them were singing with her.

'It's all right in the summertime,
In the summertime, it's lovely . . .'

There was a sudden hush as the door opened. Jody stood there, scowling.

'Shut that bloody row,' he said. 'Can't 'ear meself think.'

One of the younger girls, whose bright golden hair took its colour from a bottle, spoke up boldly.

'No law agin it, is there?'

'Never you mind what law there is and what law there ain't,' he growled. 'I've a right to me peace and quiet.'

'Try cotton-wool in yer ears – plenty of room for it!' Clemence returned. Jody glared.

'Don't give me none of your cheek!'

'Why?' she said innocently. 'It's a lot prettier than yours.'

For a moment their eyes clashed, hers defiant, his menacing. Then he withdrew his gaze. All right, milady, he thought. Put me down in front of the others, give me your lip – old Ikey won't sack you so long as you turn out the work. But I'll be even with you; you see if I won't. Abruptly he turned and went out. Clemence met glances of astonishment and admiration.

'That's all right then,' she said, resuming her buttonholing. 'If we want to sing we bloody well sing.'

'Ark at Lady Muck!' sneered a thin, bitter-faced woman. 'Nice to be independent. Some can't afford to.'

'Oh, there's always another job round the corner,' Clemence replied blithely, unaware of the resentment she was arousing in those for whom there was no other job, and never would be.

By the end of that week she was seriously thinking of looking for another one herself. For six nights she had not been home before nine o'clock, after a hurried frightening journey through narrow streets where drunkards were propped against walls or huddled on doorsteps, shouting insults to any unattended woman who passed them. Bella's placid temper was strained by the time Clemence arrived to collect the children, who had to be wakened and were consequently fretful.

And Clemence herself was tired out, sturdy as she was, by those long tedious hours of sewing in a cramped position by bad light, in an atmosphere cold, stuffy and foetid. Buttonholing, a pleasant little sewing-job normally, became monotonous to screaming-point. Several of the women were friendly to her, particularly the dark girl, Grace, who had sat next to her on the first day. Grace had come up from Hertfordshire with the impression that work and good wages were to be had for the asking in London; now she was near starving and had the hectic colour and painful cough of the consumptive.

All the girls exuded the miasma of the unwashed, but on

some mornings Clemence had noticed a powerful waft of sickly scent mingling with it. It came from Liz, the brazen-haired girl. Though Liz could not have been more than twenty she had heavy bags under her eyes and the exhausted look common to most of the work-girls. On the Friday morning Clemence saw her showing a ring around, a piece of cheap paste jewellery. The girls were giggling over it and something was said which Clemence didn't catch.

'Is it your birthday, then, Liz?' she asked innocently. Liz threw her head back with a shriek of laughter.

'My birthday! Cor love us! Does yer Ma know you're out, kid?'

Clemence was mystified. 'I thought it was a present, that's all.'

'Present my foot! Yer don't get somethin' for nothin' in this world.' She took up her sewing, her thin shoulders still shaking with mirth.

To the girl next to her she was saying 'Didn't 'alf earn it, though – one of them floggers. All right when they want you to do it to them, but t'other way round, you can keep it.' To Clemence this meant nothing.

'Whatever did I say?' she whispered to Grace, 'I thought it was a present, honest I did.'

Grace bent over her work to whisper back. 'It was from a man, Clem.'

'A sweetheart?'

'A man she'd *been* with, silly. Last night. We most of us do it so we can live. They gives us money or things we can sell, like that ring. But it ain't 'alf 'ard work after a long day, and we gets bitter cold and soaked through, waitin' about for 'em.'

Clemence stared at her, horrified. All through her child-hood she had seen prostitutes in their fourth-hand finery, scarecrow figures with rouged faces, standing patiently in alcoves like cab-horses at a rank, or guiding drunken men back to their rooms. Her mother, who had a particularly caustic tone for lapses from virtue, had explained to her that these were not like other women, and must never be ap-

125

proached or spoken to. It was impossible to associate them with her workmates, to imagine them, when they left here, going to . . . a memory came back to her of the scufflings and creakings and giggles she had heard, uncomprehending, from her parents' bed. For all her rendering of risqué songs Clemence was really very innocent. She felt a burning sense of shame – for them, for herself, as though she had been rolled in the gutter.

Several times a day Jody came up, in his capacity as 'master', to inspect the girls' work. To three very young ones who were learning the trade he was brutally sarcastic. When one began to cry he slapped her face for allowing the tears to fall on her work. To the girls with any pretensions to good looks, Grace and Liz, he spoke banteringly, lingering behind them with a hand wandering round the backs of their collars, and occasionally down the fronts. Liz bridled and preened herself, but Grace froze until he went away.

One young woman was a Russian immigrant, Vera, who spoke very little English. To her Jody shouted as though she were deaf as well as foreign, yelling 'Stupid cow!' into her uncomprehending face. But he was polite to Mrs. Aarons, the machinist, a woman of few words who ignored the others as far as possible and was in turn ignored by them. She was better paid than they were, and acted as instructor to new hands. Jody, Clemence gathered, was not Jewish, but from somewhere called Birmingham, which accounted for his peculiarly ugly accent.

It was through Jody that Clemence learnt a fact of life that shocked her almost as much because it showed up her own ignorance as because it was in itself terrible. Passing Liz one afternoon, he enquired: 'How's the kid?'

'Same as usual,' Liz returned, biting off a thread. 'Never stops yellin'. Drives me Ma crazy, 'e does. Not surprisin', though really, when you think.'

Jody agreed uninterestedly that it wasn't, and passed on. When he had gone Clemence took the first opportunity of saying, 'I didn't know you'd a baby, Liz.'

126

Liz raised plucked eyebrows. 'Well, I 'ave,' she said shortly.

Clemence persisted in social chat. 'Is he like you?'

Liz gave a shriek of laughter which was not wholly mirthful. 'Like me! That's good, that is. 'E's the spittin' image of my bruvver, if yer want to know.'

Clemence's puzzled face sent Liz into further transports. When she recovered she explained patiently, as to a small child: 'E's its farver, see? Our Fred's my kid's farver.'

Seeing that she had really shocked the younger girl, she went on more kindly: 'It's nothing special, in places like we live in, yer know. Six of us to a room, there were, till Dad passed away. Well, I mean, when fings is like that somefing's bound to 'appen, ain't it? Only 'uman nature. Some girls, it's their farvers, others it's like me and our Fred. And sometimes it's the very young kids as gets caught. 'Least I was lucky that way.'

Mrs. Aarons stopped her machine and turned round to take part in the conversation. 'You should be ashamed, Liz Groves, talking so. If you were my girl I'd put you across my knee. That child will be corrupted soon enough without your wicked words.'

'And mazel tov to you!' Liz said pertly; but Clemence noticed that she went on with her work with head bent lower than usual, and something like a flush which owed nothing to rouge was on her cheeks.

At last, after what seemed an eternity, it was Saturday night, and the girls were to be paid. In a file they trooped down to the office where Jody was sitting at his desk. During the rest of the week he acted as presser, keeping his ironing-table in the adjoining room, where a small fire was always burning. It was his great delight to catch the girls going out to the closet in the yard, and to make obscene remarks to them. Clemence had been caught this way several times, and had given him such withering looks that he had not tried further familiarities on her.

But tonight, as he called her name, he looked her up and down with an insulting stare. When she came forward to receive her money, he took her hand in his large ugly one and pressed her wages into it, folding her fingers round the coins. His hand was damp, sticky and unpleasant; she struggled to free hers. She had been the last of the applicants, and they were alone.

'Not so fast!' he muttered, and reached out for her other hand. But she wrenched herself away and backed out, slamming the door. She could hear the oath he sent after her as she set off upstairs again to fetch her coat and bonnet.

Once there, panting, she went to the gas-lamp to count her money. Her heart seemed to stop; she felt the blood drain from her face. Eight shillings lay in her palm. Only eight shillings, for a week's sweated labour in that horrible place!

There was nothing she could do; she knew that. If only she'd had the sense to admit that she was unable to read – if only she'd taken the trouble to find out from Grace what the work-rates were! Well, it was too late now. A week of her life could be written off to the gaining of knowledge – and *what* knowledge, she thought bitterly.

As she left the building she began to sob, small dry sobs of shock and self-reproaching misery. She plodded along with her head down as the tears began to pour down her face, mingled with the rain that was driving in it.

Mean narrow streets led her the most direct way to the Whitechapel Road. A few drunks were about, but the pubs had not yet closed and the streets were quiet, except for a house in which a couple were noisily fighting. At the corner of King Street she turned left into Redman's Row, still sniffing, but buoyed up by the thought that she would never, never go near that place again. Anything – scrubbing floors, serving in a shop – anything rather than that! She began to work out a plan of action. On Monday, first thing, she would . . . Out of the darkness of a side alley came an arm, hooking itself round her neck and dragging her into the shadows. Her scream was stifled by a hand over her mouth, a hand smelling of ink and sweat; and she knew it for Jody's.

CHAPTER TEN

He dragged her along with such strength that her feet were helplessly trailing along the ground, her free arm striking him ineffectually, the other pinned by her side. He had taken his hand from her mouth, and she gave scream after scream. 'Help! Help me!'

Jody laughed. 'Nobody's going to 'ear you, darlin', and they won't interfere if they do. Screams is ten a penny in this district.' They had reached the end of the dark court, in which there was neither light nor life, only the faint shine of rain on the cobblestones. It was a place of deserted mews on one side and walled backyards on the other. Jody frog-marched her to the wall which terminated the cul-de-sac and slammed her against it, holding her arms and pressing himself against her so that she was powerless to move.

'Now,' he muttered viciously, 'we'll see if we can't tame a certain young vixen, shall we?' Sickeningly, he enclosed her mouth with his, trying to force his tongue between her clenched teeth, while he savagely wrenched her skirt up. She was wild with fear, aware of a dreadful unfamiliar pressure she could not fight. Her hat was off, fallen on the ground, the long sharp hat-pin that might have served her as a weapon was out of reach. It was awful beyond imagination, but it was true: she was going to be raped.

Thoughts flashed through her mind as though she were drowning, a memory of an old man in a theatre dressing-room and a black-clad shadowy figure at the door that she thought afterwards must have been an angel, for it was nowhere to be found afterwards: and a memory of some-body telling her what to do if she were assaulted. She was to bring her knee up sharply and – but her knees were limp and trembling, no use to her. As Jody released her mouth to give his attention to searching her body she gave one last, wild, despairing shriek.

She thought it was a delusion that she heard running footsteps coming towards them. She screamed again and Jody cursed as a masculine voice shouted: 'Hold on! hold on!'

She found the strength to fight Jody now, biting and struggling and kicking, and then he was being pulled away from her and she was free of that awful incubus, while in the darkness there were ringing blows struck and a yell of pain, a fall and the unmistakable sound of bone hitting stone.

'There,' said the masculine voice pleasantly, 'that ought to settle him, I think. Now let's cast some light on things.'

Two matches rasped ineffectively, the third took light. By its tiny flickering flame she saw a gentle, dark-bearded face that looked to her hysterical view like the face of a saint, or Jesus himself, even. His pitying eyes took in her distress and dishevelment. The match went out, and, considerately, he didn't light another, so that she might have time to straighten her clothes and recover herself.

'All right?' asked the voice from the darkness. Tremulously she answered, 'Yes, sir. Oh, sir, *thank* you –'

'Never mind about thanks,' the voice said briskly. 'I think we should leave here fairly quickly, before our friend there comes round. He hit his head a pretty nasty crack, but better safe than sorry. May I?' She felt her arm gently taken, and herself being led sedately over the stones that so recently seemed to pave the way to ruin. In a few minutes they were out in gas-lit Smith Street.

The gentleman was not Jesus, nor even a saint, judging by his correct nineteenth-century attire. He was a man of medium height, strongly built without burliness. When he turned his intelligent, kindly face to her she saw that his beard covered a clergyman's collar.

'Poor girl,' he said. 'I hope you feel better now?'

'Y-yes,' she managed to say through chattering teeth, for she had begun to shiver uncontrollably. Through ringing ears she heard him say something consoling, and felt their steps quicken. Without speaking, they walked on, Clemence half-tottering on his arm, out into the brightness of the Mile

End Road, where crowds were pouring out of pubs, leaning up against walls chattering, betting on street-corners by the toss of a coin, arguing, fighting, courting. Clemence neither saw nor heard them. She was clearly conscious of nothing until she found herself being propelled up some steps into a warm, lighted room.

It was like Heaven after a taste of Hell. A cheerful fire burned in a marble surround, a leather armchair stood beside it. Into this Clemence was placed by her protector. She looked wonderingly round the room: the table laden with books and papers, the plain, old-fashioned furnishings, the framed texts, the imposing pictures, which all seemed to be of Scriptural subjects. Over the mantelpiece was a large oleograph of Christ Healing the Sick. It was all so different from the scene she had just left that she felt tears coming on again. As her lip began to tremble, she bit it firmly. The old trick worked; instead, she bestowed on her rescuer a sunny smile.

'Coo,' she said, 'that was a near thing, wasn't it.'

· · · · · ·

When she had avidly disposed of a cup of hot chocolate she learnt that she was on the premises of the Hope Mission, which was employed in spiritual and temporal rescue work in the Whitechapel and Spitalfields area.

'You're not the same as the Army, are you?' she asked, imagining her rescuer standing on a street corner playing a tambourine and singing *Washed in the Blood of the Lamb*. He laughed, and said they left that sort of thing to General Booth. He was the Mission pastor, Martin Blackwood, he told her. A tall, sweet-faced woman, very plainly dressed, joined them, and was introduced as Sister Felicity, his senior helper. 'My curate, I call her,' he said, smiling, 'but she is much more; mother confessor, nurse, accountant, among other invaluable functions. And now tell us how you came to be in such danger tonight.'

Clemence told them everything, with complete frankness. Mr. Blackwood was the sort of person one seemed to have known all one's life. Their sympathetic faces registered no shock when they heard about her experience in music-hall, though they exchanged a significant glance which said 'Here is a body and soul in mortal danger.' When she reached the sweat-shop episode, and the events of the night, Sister Felicity indignantly declared that she would report Jody to the police as an attempted rapist, before he could ruin other girls; but Mr. Blackwood pointed out that he would certainly deny everything, and that the police had enough trouble in the district without investigating a crime which had *not* been committed. Sister Felicity subsided, but the light of battle was in her eye; before she was much older some of the case-histories of Clemence's fellow-workers would be receiving her attention.

When the story was finished, Mr. Blackwood lit a pipe and gazed thoughtfully upon Clemence through the smoke.

'And now the question is what we're going to do with you,' he said.

''Spose so. I can't go back *there*, that's for certain. And I've got to work to keep my two kids. Oh, I'll find something, sir, don't you worry.'

Mr. Blackwood rose. 'Sister, will you come into the vestry for a moment, please? We shall not leave you alone for long, Miss Moffat.'

In the small vestry the two helpers confronted one another, the same thought in their minds and the same words on their lips; they had worked together so long that they had an almost marital rapport.

'This child must be saved.' He was the first to speak. 'She is pretty, lively and intelligent. Providence shielded her tonight, but there will be a next time, and a next. I believe her story implicitly. She is innocent as few are, alas, who come into our care.'

'An apprenticeship, perhaps?' the Sister suggested. 'She could be articled to some respectable milliner or dressmaker away from this area.'

'Then she would be parted from her brother and sister.'

'Of course. No, it must be nearer. I wonder –'

132

Mr. Blackwood's eyes brightened. 'Now I know exactly what you're going to say. We can use her here! She can become a force for good in the land, a worker in Our Lord's pastures! Why else was she sent to us?'

The same idea had certainly hovered in Sister Felicity's mind, but she had decided not to utter it. Now it was out, and she could only agree. Out of their funds, some of which were supplied by the Pastor's private income, Clemence could be engaged as a junior helper on the practical side of their work, assisting in households where help was needed, visiting the old and sick, caring for the Chapel and its furnishings. There were a hundred uses for her, they agreed. Her life would be filled with good works, there would be neither time nor opportunity for temptation.

It was a splendid plan; only two flaws in it caused Sister Felicity anxiety. The first was that her woman's instinct detected in Clemence's big blue eyes, clear pools of innocence, a sprite of mischief; and another dimpling at the corner of her full mouth. Unless Sister Felicity was much mistaken – and she had spent many years in the field of sociology – this was not a girl who would be content with a life of high thoughts and plain living; far, far otherwise.

And the second flaw was that in Sister Felicity's noble heart a pang of common, human jealousy struck at the thought of a woman so much younger and prettier than herself being constantly in the Pastor's company. Not, of course, that she had any but the purest thoughts of him, or he of her. But he *was* a bachelor, not yet thirty-five, and she a spinster, only two – no, to be honest, three – years older. Sometime, if the Lord chose . . . She put the unworthy thought behind her, and, calm and smiling, preceded Mr. Blackwood into the room where Clemence waited.

The scheme was a success. Clemence was delighted. Her wage enabled her to give Bella four shillings a week for feeding the children – as much as the rent of her room – and left something over for treats. She had no food to buy: it was provided free by the Mission. She was too young to be depressed by the many sad cases she saw there, young enough to be excited and gratified by work in which she got so much praise and thanks. One day, when time offered, Sister Felicity was going to teach her to read and write; already she could make out the texts in big Gothic letters, entwined with briar roses and ivy, which hung on the Mission walls. 'THOU – GOD – SEEST – ME.' It was her greatest triumph.

The Pastor congratulated himself on having gained a most valuable worker, strong, enthusiastic, energetic and honest. He asked to be taken to her home, and was warmly received there with Bella's best tea-things and the drawn-threadwork cloth her mother had embroidered. Sophy, an accomplished flirt at twelve, perched herself unasked on his knee, and Charlie talked to him gravely about books and history. Ill-health and the lack of playmates had made Charlie into a bookworm. His little pale face was now disfigured by steel spectacles; everything happened to Charlie.

Mr. Blackwood regarded him with pity, but it was Sister Felicity who did something practical about him. Twice a year the Missionaries organised a seaside treat for poor and deserving children in the neighbourhood, carefully sifting the eligible from the cadgers, for this was not a mere day excursion but a whole week by the seaside, at Broadstairs, where Sister's cousin Mrs. Foster threw open her large Georgian house to a dozen undersized and under-privileged children, most of whom had never seen the sea. Charlie, of course, was eminently eligible. He knew all about the sea, of course; he was even a little blasé about it when discussing the holiday with other children. But inwardly he seethed with excitement.

It was decided that Clemence herself should accompany the party; for she too had never seen the sea. Even the train journey was exciting, so much so that several children were sick. She was prepared and mopped them up philosophically.

It was a bright Spring day when they emerged from the station at Broadstairs, and found themselves standing near the top of a steep hilly street. And at the bottom of the street, where the houses stopped, sapphire-blue and dazzling

134

gold, stretching to infinity, was The Sea. Clemence felt a lump of emotion come into her throat. Cries of 'Cor!' 'Ow, look!' Ain't it lovely!' and the like caused passers-by to smile. But Charlie, the blasé, who could tell you the names of all the rivers in England and all the Oceans of the world and had seen pictures of Drake at Plymouth and Nelson at Trafalgar, Charlie came to his sister's side and slipped his hand into hers. Behind the thick spectacles his eyes were blurred, and he said nothing.

Clemence stayed with them that night, calming the over-wrought, dosing the queasy, and cleaning up those whose condition was not likely to appeal to Mrs. Foster's maids (who threatened every year to leave if Them Slum Kids returned once more). Then, when they were all in bed and had been individually kissed, she put on her bonnet and went out, alone.

You could go out alone in Broadstairs, the maids had told her. It wasn't like London, where a girl took her virtue in her hands every time she crossed the road. The cobbled streets were quiet. A returning fisherman passed her with his catch and gave her a civil Good Night, startling her so much that he was past before she could reply. People didn't greet you like that in London.

Even the inns looked respectable, and had curious names like The Tartar Frigate, down by the jetty. There was a lovely smell of salt and seaweed; she put her head back and breathed in lungfuls of it.

'It's like I hadn't never breathed before,' she thought. She took off her bonnet and let the breeze play with her hair, disturbing the thick knot of it and tousling her fringe.

She walked to the end of the old jetty, and turned to look at the town in the apricot light of sunset; the strange old figure of a man carved in wood, that she thought must have come off a ship, for she'd seen things like that at the Docks; the house high up on the cliff where, Mrs. Foster had said, the writer Charles Dickens had lived. It was because of books he had written that Mrs. Foster had devoted so much time and money to poor children, and Sister Felicity too. A

135

strange yearning, almost painful, came over Clemence; something she couldn't understand. She longed to be wiser, cleverer, to be able to read such books and know what life was all about. Here, by the infinite sea, she, the pertly cocky and self-satisfied, felt suddenly reduced in size to a tiny figure, ignorant and unimportant.

And yet it was all so beautiful that on the whole she had never been so happy in her life. A tremendous peace descended on her, borne on the roll and crash of the waves. It was like soft, continuous applause. Contemptuously she looked back at her theatre life.

'Pooh!' she said to the wooden figurehead. 'Audiences! you can keep 'em.'

The beautiful week was over far too soon. The children, their pallor overlaid with colour from the sun and the wind, were back in their noisome homes, and Clemence had come out of her dream and returned to work. In the little Mission Hall in Mile End Road she stood sensibly overalled by a large steaming vat of soup, which she was ladling out to a hungry queue, with encouraging cries borrowed from the fairground barker.

'Roll up, me lucky lads! One at a time please, or you'll be killed in the rush. Come and take hadvantage of this hunrepeatable hoffer! Made by me own fair 'ands this very afternoon. Not tuppence a plate – not a penny a plate – but Free!' One bold applicant was encouraged by her lively manner to slip an arm round her waist and steal a kiss, for which he got a ringing slap in the face.

'Sauce!' she said indignantly. Martin Blackwood, watching, smiled and shook his head. 'Clemence, Clemence, you're born to trouble,' he thought. And yet – so bright, so lovely ... so strong.

Sometimes Clemence would go round for tea to the Pastor's rooms, round the corner in Bancroft Street. He occupied the upper floor of a small, shabby house, cheerlessly furnished by his deeply religious landlady, who was above such worldly things as comfortable chairs and hearth-rugs, and even glanced with suspicion on pictures. The prevalent note in the living-room was a bilious dark green, its most conspicuous piece of furniture a mean-looking couch upholstered in horsehair, on which Clemence sat in a continuous state of slithering, while the host occupied a chair which would have done credit to the Holy Inquisition.

'Why don't you make that woman give you a proper chair?' she demanded. The Pastor smiled.

'My dear child, I really spend so little time sitting in it that a more luxurious one would be wasted on me. Comfort is only for the lazy.'

Clemence shrugged. 'Strikes me she don't look after you like she should. Not when you've been used to something different.' She pointed to a framed photograph on the mantelpiece of Mr. Blackwood's mother, a lady of calm and saintly appearance clad in silk of obvious richness, with a fluffy jabot of lace at her august throat. '*She* wouldn't of liked to see you like this.'

'Wouldn't *have*,' he corrected automatically. 'My dear mother? I expect you're right.' The small sigh that escaped him made her cock her head like an inquisitive robin.

'Very fond of her, were you?' The Pastor looked taken aback.

'Really, I don't . . . well, yes, I suppose I was. But I saw far less of her than most children, so perhaps there was not the closeness . . . My father died when I was a small child, and my mother thought it her duty to bring me up as rigidly as possible. She sent me to boarding-school when I was only six, a school up in Yorkshire. I didn't come home very often.' His wistful gaze was fixed on the repellent paper fan which occupied the grate in place of a fire, seeing the cold, bare schoolroom, the bleak view of moorland from the windows, the iron beds in the dormitory; hearing his young self sobbing with his head under the pillow.

'You didn't like it there?'

'I – no. No. I don't think I knew what happiness was until I went to University.'

Clemence's eyes were round with awe. 'Was you at college, then?'

'*Were* you, not was you. Yes, at Magdalen. It's one of the most beautiful of Oxford colleges, on the bridge. I rowed for Oxford, you know.' He pointed out a group photograph of young men, grim-faced, heavily moustached, with an imposing set of oars. 'We beat Cambridge that year. There was glory for you!'

Clemence said nothing. She admired him so much, but his world was beyond her comprehension. Sometimes he seemed so old and staid, sometimes no older than a boy. Her gaze returned to the photograph.

'You was lucky, having all that education. Don't I wish I had it!'

'Your education is life itself, my child.'

'That's all very well, but it won't make me a lady. I want to be – oh, I don't know *what* I want to be! A famous Something, that's all . . .'

He quoted at her 'Be good, sweet maid, and let who will be clever.'

'Can't you be both, then?' she returned pertly. And indeed, it was a continual puzzle to her that such good ladies as Sister Felicity (who, it turned out, was a Honourable) should wear such ugly clothes and not bother much about their hair. She hoped that a virtuous life would not have the same effect on her.

The summer of 1899 was the most pleasant Clemence had ever known. Her landlord, Mr. O'Rourke, let her have the small back room on the landing above the Clicketts for a rent of two shillings a week. The scandal of Marianne's suicide had been the only blot on the Moffats' record, and he was pleased to have decent tenants instead of what he might have got in their place. The younger children liked the experience of living under the dormer roof; from the built-out attic window they could see over the tops of the houses in Whitechapel High Street to the masts of the Docks. In the early evening flocks of starlings flew over, a pattern of black dots, twittering on their mysterious journey to their Westminster roosts. Inquisitive sparrows discovered that crumbs miraculously appeared on the window-sill each day, especially for their benefit, and became hand-tame in no time.

'You could see the sea,' said Charlie wistfully, 'if it wasn't for the houses. I like it when the gulls come over.' Sophy satisfied her housewifely instincts by growing a geranium in a pot; it made their room look almost like the country.

Incredible that war was brewing again in Africa. Lord Kitchener had smashed the power of the Mahdi at the Battle of Omdurman in the previous year, but the Queen firmly backed her Government in believing that Britain should regain the Transvaal. By autumn she was blessing her departing soldiers, thousands of Tommy Atkinses in khaki, so many of whom would never come home again. Death by Boer bullets or the terrible enteric fever waited for them, as war-zeal invaded the concert platform and the music-hall, and Clemence went about her work singing *Jolly good luck to the girl who loves a soldier* and *Goodbye, Dolly I must leave you*. Every family seemed to have a soldier son, father, brother or husband; as Clemence said, it seemed downright unfair to have nobody to worry about.

As the days and the news grew darker, the lack was supplied. One night Bella tapped at her door and entered quietly. She jerked her head towards the children's beds, and Clemence nodded.

'They're off all right.' Bella drew up a chair.

'I wanted a bit of a word with you, Clem.' Her usually cheerful face was unsmiling. 'You noticed Sam lately – anything different?'

Clemence couldn't say she had. He was seldom in when she got home, risking the hazards of the 'night-cab driver' life for the extra money it brought.

Bella's voice shook. ''E told me tonight. I thought 'e didn't look 'isself, but I never thought it was *that*.'

'That' had only one meaning. Shocked, Clemence stared at her.

'Oh, no! Oh, Bella!'

'It's the pain. 'E can't 'ide it no more. That's why 'e told me.' She hid her face in her hands and began to sob. Clemence embraced her, making little soothing sounds, until Bella recovered sufficiently to straighten and mop her eyes.

'And the thing I can't get over is that 'e don't worry about 'imself – only about Inkerman. "What will they do with 'im when I'm gone?" 'e keeps asking. Well, Clem, you and I know the answer to that one.'

She did. Everybody did. The horse too old to work, even in a humbler line of business, would be taken along to Garratt Lane, Wandsworth, his mane ignominiously shaven so that he could never be resold; there, standing humble and blindfolded, he would be poleaxed. In a matter of hours he would be only meat for cats, fat for candles, bone-manure for gardens. Lucky the horse that was 'retired' to die in meadow or stable, full of years.

Clemence's face flamed with anger and her fists clenched. 'Oh, that woman!' she said. 'I could kill her, that Miss de Thing Dad worked for that never came near us afterwards. *She* could have taken Inkerman to that hunt place of hers. Rich bitch!'

'Now, Clem, that's no way to talk. Won't do no good to Sam. Can't you think of something?' Her eyes pleaded. Clemence thought, hard; inspiration came.

'Tell you what, Bella. If – when Sam can't drive him no more, I'll pay for his food, and see he's kept all right. That'll give us time to think. I've got it! I'll speak to the Pastor.'

But for once Mr. Blackwood couldn't help. His country connections were few and his interest in animal welfare luke-warm; people, he considered, were his province. At his suggestion Clemence walked to Soho to see the Cab Drivers' Association, where a starch-collared lady promised to look into the case of Mr. Clickett, who might well be a candidate for the £12 a year grant to men too old or infirm to work, but seemed to think Clemence quite mad when she asked for help for a horse. The Royal Society for the Prevention of Cruelty to Animals was sympathetic, but pointed out that cruelty was not involved, and that there were a great number of horses in London.

That night she went to the mews in Chicksand Street where Inkerman was stabled. He knew her call, and whinnied as

140

she approached. There was always an apple for him in her pocket. He accepted it graciously, munching while she stroked his nose. Though fed well, he was thin, the ribs showing beneath the rough brown coat; six days a week tells on a horse.

'Whatever are we going to do with you, old boy?' she asked him. His soulful eyes beamed intelligently, but no mystic communication came from them.

'I'm losing me powers,' she said. 'When I was Sophy's age I could read teacups, all sorts of things. Must be growing up that does it. D'you know what my Dad used to say to me, and I never forgot it? "There's a way round most things," he used to say. And there is, too, I do believe. Come on now, what's the way round this one?'

Inkerman shut his eyes and appeared to be either in deep thought or asleep.

His master deteriorated fast. From a wiry little man he had become almost fleshless, his brown face deadly pale, his eyes sunk back in his head. Soon he was unable to leave his bed. Bella took turns with Polly and Amy in nursing him, for he was a trying patient. Worry for his horse alternated in his tormented mind with worry for the British troops in South Africa, the armies besieged in Ladysmith, in Kimberley and Mafeking. 'They oughter send Kitchener!' he repeated, over and over. 'Kitchener and Bobs, them's the men they want.' His thoughts wandered back to his soldiering days in the Crimea, to Cardigan and Raglan and the terrible mistaken Charge. 'It was the 'orses, Clem!' he would mutter, catching her sleeve with a clawlike hand. 'I could bear to 'ear me pals scream, but not them innocent nags. They didn't call me soft for it, neither, Clem, for they loved their 'orses like women . . .'

'Never mind,' she murmured comfortingly, 'they're gone now, gone long ago. You tell me about Miss Nightingale instead.'

His skeletal face would light up as he told of the figure flitting through field-hospital wards by night, a lamp in its gentle hand, of men dying comforted as if their mother had been beside them; 'but she could be a Tartar, too, could

141

Miss Nightingale, if them young nurses put a foot wrong. The Angel of the Crimea, they called 'er . .' He rambled on until merciful sleep came to him. Once he asked for his old sword. It had been pawned long ago, but Bella told him it was away being cleaned; he never asked for it again.

Most of all he raved of Inkerman, sometimes thinking him a foal again on a blanket by the fire, sometimes urging him on the last mile home, or praising him for a good quick journey. And then dreaded consciousness would come to remind him that his own death sentence would also be Inkerman's; the degrading sentence of the slaughterhouse. Slow tears trickled down his cheeks. The women had no comfort for him; they could only turn away.

The crisis came in England's Black Week, the week in December when three of her Generals were defeated, and Ladysmith seemed lost. They kept the bad news from Sam, but he seemed to sense it, and to fail with England's hopes. He no longer rambled, but lay, silently nursing his pain, staring at the ceiling. Outside the worst fog for years hid the houses. The doctor struggled through it to answer Bella's summons. By the bedside he shook his head.

'There's nothing I can do – apart from giving him morphia.'

He prescribed the dose, and left.

Clemence, upstairs, had been preparing the children's supper. Suddenly, answering some signal in her brain, she took down her old cloak from the door and put it on.

'I'm going out for a bit, Sophy!'

'Clem, you *can't*! It's a regular peasouper!'

'I can see that, can't I, but I've got to go, love. Don't let the bacon get all burnt up.' And she was gone, feeling her way along the wall of the Court, between the posts at the end, across Montague Street, going slowly and carefully. Up Casson Street she went, losing direction once or twice; then through the choking reek of the fog the warm sweet smell of horses told her that she was in Chicksand Street and almost at the mews. She had no idea what she was doing there. A door opened, letting out a flood of golden light.

The stableman who lived above stood there with a lantern.

'Who's that?'

'It's me, Tom,' she answered, moving into the lantern's orbit. His mouth fell open. 'My Gawd,' he said. 'Who'd have believed it! What you doin' 'ere, Miss Moffat?'

She gave a small embarrassed laugh. 'I know, I want me head seeing to. I came to see if Inkerman was all right and tight.'

Tom still looked as if a beam had fallen on his head. He came out into the yard.

'He's gone, miss.'

'Gone? Gone where?'

'Dead. Dropped down stone dead an hour since, when I come to bed 'em down for the night. No cause that I could see – it was just as if 'is 'eart stopped.'

There was a silence as Clemence tried to take in what she had been told. Then she said: 'Can I see him?'

Tom went before her with the lantern into Inkerman's stall. The horse lay on the straw-strewn floor, on his side, in a relaxed position, as if he had suddenly fallen asleep rolling in a meadow.

Clemence hardly remembered how she got back. She went straight to the Clicketts' door. Bella let her in with a drawn face.

'It's come, Clem,' she said.

Clemence went to Sam's bedside and knelt beside it. 'Can you hear me, Sam?' she asked. 'Nod if you can.' Painfully the head moved up and down.

'I've got good news for you. Ever such good news. You won't never need to worry about Inkerman going to the knacker's, Sam.'

The dry lips moved with difficulty.

'They've . . . taken 'im to the country?'

'That's it. They come for him tonight. He – he'll be there by now.'

A smile of singular beauty transformed the dying man's face. He laid his hand upon hers, and died.

CHAPTER ELEVEN

Clemence would never, if she lived to be a hundred, forget December 1899. That sad Christmas Eve Sam was buried, and Bella left Black Lion Yard to go and live with Polly.

'If I stayed I'd see 'im everywhere,' she told Clemence. 'Thirty years we'd 'ave been married, if 'e'd lived. I don't like to leave you and the nippers, Clem, but I've got to go, and Polly wants me now she's on the way with 'er third.' Sadly, affectionately, they kissed and hugged each other, and Clemence tried to tell Bella something of her love and gratitude, but could only weep.

The Moffats spent Christmas Day at the Pastor's lodgings. It was not a merry occasion but it was better than staying in their attic, conscious of the empty place downstairs which would soon be filled by strangers. In the morning they attended service at the Mission Chapel, returning to Bancroft Street for a midday dinner cooked and served with a maximum of ungraciousness by Mr. Blackwood's landlady, who strongly resented having extra mouths to feed. She was given to uttering her thoughts aloud, a habit which did not enhance her popularity. Clemence distinctly heard herself described as 'flighty' and 'no better than she should be, to judge by looks', and Sophy as 'a noisy brat'. But the dinner was free, and they were glad of it, and of the quiet afternoon looking at copies of *Sunday at Home*.

The fog, which had lifted slightly as if making a concession to Christmas, fell again, a thicker pall than ever, making Charlie cough incessantly on their journey home. When they got there he was sick: 'waste of a good dinner!' said Clemence, and put him straight to bed with a stone hot-water bottle.

In the morning he was feverish. Clemence felt his forehead. It was dry and burning, and his lips were cracked. His face had the bluish tinge she remembered from his babyhood. A dreadful apprehension fell like a lead weight on her heart. Funny, she thought as she went for the doctor, all the songs and that talk about your heart like it was your brain, which it's not, and yet when something bad happens you feel it just *there*. Her heart was beating very fast, though she could only make slow progress through the foggy streets.

The doctor was not pleased to be called out on Boxing Day.

'Are you sure it isn't just one of his attacks?' he asked Clemence irritably.

She was firm. 'No, it's not, I've never seen him like this. Oh, do come, please, doctor! He's ever so ill, I know he is!'

Growling, the doctor got his coat and bag, jammed his head into a woollen Balaclava, and set out with her, neither of them speaking. But when he saw the sick boy his manner changed.

'Good thing you called me. Your brother must go to hospital at once, or I shan't answer for the consequences.' Her mouth fell open.

'Hospital!'

'That's what I said. He's in the grip of an extremely serious asthmatic attack and needs professional nursing. If you'll get him dressed and warmly wrapped up I'll try to find a cab in this confounded fog.' He stumped out, and Clemence struggled to get some clothes on to Charlie, who was quite unable to help her, then took the blanket off his bed and wrapped it round him. Sophy watched with anxious eyes.

'Is Charlie very ill, Clem?'

Clemence nodded, tight-lipped.

'He should never have gone out yesterday, never. I knew it, all upset as he was about Sam, and then the fog. I'm a stupid bloody fool, and you can forget I said that, Soph, but I had to. Oh my God, how long is that doctor going to be?'

It seemed hours before he came back to say that a cab was standing at the entrance to the Court. Between them they carried Charlie downstairs – he was only a light weight – and got him outside and into the cab, which the doctor ordered to drive to the London Hospital. There, in that great frightening place with its uneasy antiseptic smell, Clemence was told to wait while Charlie was put to bed in a ward. She sat in the waiting-hall, her eyes roving round the cold tiled walls, the benches, where some sick-looking people awaited their call to see a doctor, the depressing bath-chairs and spinal carriages waiting for patients who couldn't walk. All waiting, she thought. All waiting for something, and it won't be nice when it comes. It's as though the whole world's gone dark and the sun's dead. That's it, the sun's dead, like Sam and Inkerman and . . . she put the next thought from her.

Seeing a woman enter with a trolley of tea, she went and got herself a cup, but it tasted of nothing. She wished she could read, so that the time would pass quicker; there were some newspapers and magazines lying about. She wondered if Sophy was all right at home, prayed that she was not setting her dress accidentally on fire.

At last a starched nurse rustled up to her and conducted her briskly to a lift, which bore them upstairs. The nurse preceded her into a long ward full of high narrow beds. The people in them all looked alike to her; she had to look twice at Charlie to make sure it was him. They had taken his spectacles off and folded them neatly on the table by the bed. Somehow that distressed her more than the sight of the purplish face on the stark white pillow, and the stertorous breathing.

'There, you see,' said the nurse in that bright sensible voice peculiar to nurses, 'your brother's quite comfortable, and there's nothing you can do for him, so run along home, there's a good girl. You can come back tomorrow between two and three in the afternoon.'

Charlie lay in the high narrow bed for five days. When Clemence called on the fifth, which was New Year's Eve, she was met at the door of the ward by the lady in the special cap with the frill, who wore a darker dress than the nurses and was revered as Sister.

'Will you come into my office a moment, Miss Moffat?' she asked. They went into a small sparklingly clean room with a small fire in it. 'Do sit down,' Sister invited. Clemence began to shiver.

'It's Charlie, isn't it,' she said flatly. 'He's not going to get better.'

Sister laid a gentle hand on her arm.

'I'm afraid it's rather more than that, my dear,' she said.

For the first time in her life Clemence fainted. She came to with her head between her knees, hearing the rattle of glass and bottle.

'Drink this,' Sister said, putting a glass in her hand. It gave off the pungent odour of brandy. Clemence shut her eyes and swallowed it at one gulp.

'Perhaps you would like to see him,' said Sister, 'if it won't distress you too much?' Clemence shook her head, and followed her into the ward, to a bed which had screens round it.

.   .   .   .   .   .

Everybody was very kind to her. At the Mission, where she resolutely went on working, people whose faces she didn't even know came up to speak to her and condole. Her courage caused general admiration. She bought a length of material and made up black frocks for herself and Sophy, but that was her only concession to mourning. When she came to the Mission red-eyed in the mornings everybody tactfully ignored it. 'You've got to go on, if the sky falls,' she said.

One practical problem she had to tackle was that of Sophy. The child couldn't be allowed to come home from school to an empty room, and stay there by herself when Clemence was out. She was twelve, docile and pretty, at times looking like a paler copy of Clemence, and she could sew reasonably well. She was not going to learn much more at school (Charlie had been the clever one) and might as well leave.

'I've got it!' said Clemence. 'Madame Billings.' On a bitter January day of 1900 (Charlie had not seen the turn of the century) she tramped up to Islington, the address she remembered from her mother's stories of her girlhood. And, astonishingly, after all the years Madame Billings and her establishment were still there, Madame portly as a pouter-pigeon, beautifully coiffured and made up, and smelling delicately of violet scent.

She welcomed Clemence graciously. 'My dear, I should have known you anywhere for Miss Dumas's daughter. I shall never forget that pretty girl. Well, well, a pleasant surprise.' She sat Clemence down in her neat parlour above the shop, and listened to her story, her eyes filling with sympathetic tears at its last chapter.

The idea of adding Sophy to her staff of apprentices seemed to enchant her. 'I'm sure she is a charming and ladylike young creature,' she said, 'if her mother and sister are anything to go by.'

'She's a lot more ladylike than me,' Clemence admitted frankly, 'she's been to school, which is more than I have.'

Mrs. Billings led her downstairs and showed her the workroom, where four pretty girls were sewing and chattering. Ravishing hats perched like tropical birds on stands, charming enough to have drawn down the stone nymphs who adorned the Grand Theatre across the road.

Clemence was delighted and reassured, particularly when Madame told her that the mother of one of the girls, a highly respectable widow, was prepared to take a young woman lodger for a very reasonable rent. 'After all, the girls are out all day, and eat very little,' she added.

Clemence thought privately that Sophy would certainly prove the exception to the rule so far as eating went, but that would have to sort itself out. They had reached the hall again, and she was extending her hand to Madame Billings when that lady said:

'Oh, and about the premium.'

'Premium?'

'Yes, my dear, I have to ask for fifty pounds in advance to cover the four-year period. This is a very superior establishment, you see.' She beamed upon the crestfallen Clemence. Fifty pounds! Where in the world could she lay hands on fifty pounds? Fifty pence, more like. She hesitated; it was too good a chance to get Sophy settled. Somehow it must be found. Then she said, 'I'll do my best, Madame. And I'll bring her to see you on Sunday, like you said.'

They shook hands and parted, Madame cordially waving from the door as Clemence trudged away down Upper Street. The girl's downcast expression had not escaped her, but she probably had a gentleman friend who would oblige. All these girls had. She returned to the parlour and rang for tea and anchovy toast.

The only gentleman friend in Clemence's life was Martin Blackwood. She went to him unhesitatingly. He was at home, working with Sister Felicity on the Mission accounts, but when he gathered from Clemence's hints that her business was personal, he shut the ledger.

'We'll finish it off in the morning, Sister, shall we? I can see that Clemence wants to have a little talk. Perhaps you would like Sister to stay, Clemence?' But Clemence hesitated, and Sister took her cue for leaving.

'Whatever the trouble, I hope it will soon clear up, my dear,' she said. 'Enough has come your way lately.'

'Born to it, I reckon, like the Pastor says,' Clemence answered cheerfully. When they were alone she took the proffered chair and began. 'It's like begging, and I hate asking. But I couldn't think of anybody but you.' She launched into a colourful account of her visit, imitating Madame Billings to the life. 'And after all that buttering-up, she asks me for fifty pounds! Well, do I look as if I'd got fifty pounds tucked in me gar – pocket?'

He admitted that she didn't.

'So that's about it. If you'll lend it me I'll be thankful to you for ever after, and it *is* only lend, mind, because one of these days I'm going to be Somebody, and I'll pay you back with ten per cent on top of it!'

The Pastor laughed. 'I'll look forward to that day.'

'Then you'll do it?' she asked eagerly.

'Of course. For you. You shall take it with you when you go with Sophy.'

She began to overwhelm him with thanks, but he stopped her. 'Thank Our Lord that he has sent you friends and a solution to your difficulties. May it always be so for you.' He leant forward and gazed at her earnestly. 'For some time I have meant to have a talk with you, Clemence. Perhaps this is the moment.'

She waited. He began to fill his pipe, tamping down the tobacco, regarding the result thoughtfully, lit it and took a few puffs. Clemence wished he would get on with it, whatever it was. She'd had a long walk and wanted nothing so much as to go home and put her feet up, not to mention telling Sophy the good news. At last he spoke.

'How old are you, Clemence?'

'Eighteen next birthday – July.'

'And you've been with us over a year. I have watched you during that year, Clemence, with interest and, I may say, admiration. You are not naturally pious, I know.' Clemence wriggled slightly, hoping they were not going to talk about religion. He smiled. 'Don't worry. We are not all called to serve in the same way. But you have served manfully in yours. You have a heart that goes with your name – Clemence, clemency, kindness. You are good-humoured, intelligent, honest.' Clemence stifled a giggle, because it was beginning to sound like a dog's pedigree. 'Your care for your brother and sister has been the care of a thoroughly responsible person. On the other side of the coin, you have a hasty temper and a habit of using – shall we say – unsuitable words.'

Clemence blushed. So he *had* heard those occasional bloodies that slipped out, not to mention one or two words she'd picked up on the halls.

'And, gravest of all, you are not educated. No, I know it is no fault of yours. But would you not like to be educated, to read and write and speak as a lady should?'

'Oh, *yes*!'

He nodded gravely. 'Of course you would. Now, if you agree Sister Felicity and I will give up as much time as we can to teach you. It should not be hard, with a pupil as bright as you are.'

Glowing with gratitude and excitement, she clapped her hands together. 'Oh,' she said, 'I could – I could kiss you!'

In every life words are said which cause barriers to fall, inhibitions to crumble. These words, artlessly spoken, changed the Pastor from a fatherly clergyman to someone years younger, eager and ardent, as the young rowing Blue in the portrait must have been. He caught her hands between his in a grasp that made her wince.

'Clemence, Clem dear, won't you marry me? Oh, don't look like that, you must know I love you! I've loved you ever since that night when you came into my life like God's own sunshine. I never told you before because I hardly admitted it to myself. I thought perhaps it was wrong, a child like you, half my age. I thought – I don't know what. It doesn't matter now. Won't you give me your answer?'

For the first time in her life Clemence was literally without words. She felt as though the ceiling had collapsed on her head and knocked out of it every single sensible thought. With an effort she pulled herself together. What did ladies in plays say at moments like this? 'Sir, unhand me!' or 'This is so sudden! Pray, Mr. Montmorency, grant me leisure to reflect upon your strange proposition!' Yes, that was the line. Politely she withdrew her hands from his.

'I couldn't, not right away, sir. I didn't know, you see. I shouldn't have thought a gentleman like you would –'

'Would want you for his wife? Clemence, a moment ago you said you intended to be Somebody. What better could you do with your life than dedicate it to the service of God?'

A vision of herself in furs and diamonds flashed before Clemence's inward eye, followed by another in which she wore a saucy dress that would make Marie Lloyd green with envy, scooped low enough to make the boys whistle and pinching-tight in the waist with a pair of black French corsets underneath. Aloud she said, 'Sir, I think you're wrong, really I do. I'm not that sort of girl. I'm not a bit serious. I like a bit of fun and frolics, and I'd disgrace you.

Imagine me, a clergyman's wife! It's been all right at the Mission, and I like looking after people that's worse off than me, but do it all the time . . . well, I just couldn't.'

He came to her side, and gently tilted up her chin, looking into her eyes; just as the spaniel Sheba had looked, she thought, and reproved herself for comparing Mr. Blackwood to a dog, even a nice one.

'Well, never mind about the – shall we say the parsonical side of it,' he said. 'I'd make you a good husband, Clemence. Oh, I know my own faults. I'm weak, vacillating; selfish, very often. And I need you so much. I need your gaiety, and your beauty, and your strength. You could transform my life. And I do believe I could transform yours. Won't you say yes, dear?'

Clemence had a mad impulse to break into *Daisy, Daisy, give me your answer, do.* The words had a wild aptness: 'It won't be a stylish marriage, We can't afford a carriage.' Mr. Blackwood and herself sailing along the Mile End Road on a bicycle made for two . . . she gave an irrepressible laugh, which turned into one of those fits of giggles that beset the very young. To and fro she rocked on the horsehair sofa, tears of laughter rolling down her cheeks, her handkerchief stuffed in her mouth. She knew it was an awful thing to do but she couldn't stop it. The Pastor sat down by her side and took her in his arms, as gently as if she had been made of spun glass.

'Don't laugh at me, Clemence,' he said sadly. 'Please don't.'

His tone sobered her. She sat up, mopping her eyes, still hardly able to speak. 'It – wasn't you,' she got out between hiccups. 'I just thought of something funny.'

He shook his head reprovingly, as if to say that it was an odd time to choose. 'Be serious, now. Do you need time to think?'

'Oh, yes, please. Lots of time.' She was thinking even as she spoke; if she married him, she would have security, a home, a position in life, there'd be no more need to worry about Sophy. And even though he was so churchy he was a nice man, very kind and very brave – look how he'd rescued her that awful night. All right thinking about being a duchess or a famous actress, but life wasn't like that. A girl like her could end up on the streets, if the luck went against her. And it *had* been against her lately. Perhaps she'd be foolhardy to say no. She could jolly him along when they were married, liven him up a bit. He wasn't even all that old.

'I will think, really,' she said. 'I'll try and see it your way. It might work. And it's a great compliment, sir.'

'Oh, Clemence!' He still had an arm round her shoulders. He embraced her again, kissed her cheek and her hair, held her hand against his face and kissed the palm. She rather enjoyed the sensation; it was quite different from the horrors of Jody's attentions. She leant back and gave him an encouraging smile which showed off her dimples to advantage, offering her lips. It seemed strange to be kissing the Pastor, but if they were going to be engaged it was all right, of course. Very lightly, very chastely, he kissed her on the mouth, then clasped her tightly, and said with his lips against her hair:

'Will you make me very happy, Clemence? Will you – do something I want very much?'

Here we go, she thought. Men are all alike. Give them an inch and you're in bed before you can say Jack Robinson. Mum always said so, and she was right.

'Depends what it is,' she said coldly. She liked him less now, breathing heavily in her ear, his usually pale face flushed.

'I'll show you,' he said, in a voice quite unlike his normal one, disquieting her. He released her and went to a cupboard, painted the same depressing green as the walls. He took a bunch of keys from his pocket and unlocked it. What on earth was coming now? A top hat with a rabbit in it? Flags of All Nations in an endless string? He took something out of the cupboard. 'Can't you guess?' he asked, his voice trembling. From behind his back he produced a small, neat, triple-thonged whip.

Clemence stared at it blankly. 'What's that for?'

Suddenly he fell to his knees at her feet, clasping her legs. 'Dear, sweet, adorable Clemence, don't you understand? I want you to rule me, dominate me, punish me for all my manifold sins and wickednesses! Treat me as harshly as you like, and I'll kiss your feet for it. Beat me, flog me, Clemence!'

He tried to force the whip into her hand as she shrank back against the rail of the sofa. His face was altered, flushed and strange, his eyes wild. Into her frightened bewildered mind suddenly came some words overheard at the sweatshop: Liz saying, 'Didn't 'alf earn it, though – one of them floggers. All right when they want you to do it to them, but t'other way round, you can keep it.' Now, in a flash, she understood, though nobody had told her of the strange perversion so common in England; the desire for physical punishment born of public-school floggings, the pleasure that was only roused by pain.

He was clutching her frock, saying words that meant nothing to her. She dragged the material from his hands, pushed him violently away, so that he sprawled on the floor, staring at her wildly. She ran out of the room, caught a glimpse of the landlady's outraged face in the lobby, struggled with the catch of the front door and let herself out. Then she ran and ran, blindly making for home, unaware of the surprised looks of people in the street. She was nearly home when she realised she had left her coat behind her. Well, that was too bad, but she wasn't going back for it; never, never, never!

In the attic room she flung herself down and cried as she had not cried even for Charlie's death. Outrage, humiliation, even a kind of disappointment had more power than grief.

'Clem, Clem, what is it?' Sophy was kneeling by her, trying to quieten her. With an effort she sat up. 'Nothing. Just a – shock I had. Something I saw in the street.'

There would be no apprenticeship for Sophy now, of course. She would have to think again, try to find the child a place somewhere, anywhere away from here.

But next day a messenger-boy came to the door. He brought a parcel with her coat in it, and an envelope that held fifty golden sovereigns. There was no letter enclosed.

That Sunday Clemence and Sophy travelled by cab to Madame Billings's, their few possessions in a couple of boxes. Mum's Cupid had been carefully wrapped in a petticoat, together with the Chelsea dog.

Madame was paid, Sophy ensconced, with her landlady, in a pleasant house behind Islington Green. At the door Clemence kissed her.

'Cheer up. Let's see you smile.'

'But where are you *going*, Clem?' Sophy's lip trembled.

Where *was* she going, come to think of it? Her flight from Whitechapel had been an escape. What she needed now was a new path in life, a signpost. As if by magic, the bells of St. Mary's Church began to ring for evening service. Clemence laughed with delight.

'Remember last year's Panto, love? Dick on Highgate Hill?'

'Oh yes, and the funny cat.'

'That's right.' She struck an attitude, cupping one ear.

'Hark, trusty Pussy, don't you hear the bells?
   They're saying "Turn round, Whittington, or else –!"'
   Come, Puss, let's make our way, with footsteps bold,
   To London, where the streets are paved with gold!'

'I'll see you very soon, pet. Be good!'

She turned on her heel and stepped out briskly, her head high.

BOOK THREE: BLACK SPIRITS AND WHITE

CHAPTER TWELVE

The skies had been iron-grey all that day, with a menacing bite in the air. Clemence walked fast, thankful for even a pair of cotton gloves to keep her hands from complete numbness. She felt recklessly cheerful, setting off on this new adventure. Instinct told her to travel westwards, towards that part of London where prosperity was to be found. Everything that had happened had been for the best, after all, and here she was, exactly like a female Dick Whittington, with her little hatbox containing what clothes she possessed slung on her arm, and her purse, with its precious sovereign, her total savings, in her pocket.

She went by way of Pentonville Road, because of what her mother had told her of her parents' courtship there. In St. James's Church tower the bells had stopped; the windows were lighted and the congregation were singing a hymn. Somewhere in that churchyard did the ghost with the sad face still walk, the apparition young Marianne Dumas had seen? It was too cold to linger on the chance of seeing him. Indeed, a few flakes of snow were beginning to fall.

She decided to strike off southwards through the streets leading to Gray's Inn Road. The snow was coming thicker now. The sooner she found a night's lodging the better. For a very little money she could get a room and move on in the morning. But though lodgings were advertised here and there, the houses looked sleazy; she hurried on.

As she walked down one of the little streets a voice accosted her. On a doorstep sat an old woman, little more than a bundle of rags, so far as Clemence could see in the dim light from a distant street-lamp. A bony hand reached out.

'Spare a penny, lady! Only a penny, for Gawd's sake!'

Clemence hesitated. She had a few pence in her purse besides the sovereign – could she spare them?

The whine came again. 'Bring yer luck, dear! Pity the pore and yer'll never regret it. I've not touched a bite these two days, as Gawd's above's my witness.'

Clemence's heart was too soft to resist the appeal. She fished in her purse and put two pennies, enough for a meal, into the dirty claw.

'That's all I've got to spare, Ma. Good luck.'

Before she could move away she was grasped from behind. Her assailant wrenched the hatbox from her arm and the purse from her hand, and gave her a violent push forward. She fell full-length, hitting her head against the step with violent impact. For a moment or two she lay there, sick with pain and trembling with shock. When she managed to crawl to her feet, the beggar-woman had vanished from the doorstep; far away down the street, passing the lamp, she saw two scurrying figures, a man and a woman. She tried to set off in pursuit, but her trembling legs gave way and she sank down on the step to recover.

'Well, you're a donkey, and no mistake,' she said to herself. 'Of all the old tricks, to get done like that! Ought to be certified.' Suddenly the seriousness of her plight struck her. She was penniless; her possessions and her hatbox were gone. By now the thieves would have gone to earth, beyond finding. There was the possibility of going back to Islington and asking Sophy's landlady for shelter. But it had taken her an hour to get where she was, going the long way round by Pentonville Road, and she doubted whether she could find her way by short cuts, in the snowfall which was rapidly becoming blindingly thick. Somehow she must get indoors. There was the Salvation Army; perhaps she could find a hostel in Gray's Inn Road.

But when she reached it, at a point north of the Royal Free Hospital, the wide street presented a blank face to her. The shops were shut for Sunday, the streets deserted: only at the Hospital there was light, life and movement, and she shrank from presenting herself there. Policemen, so com-

157

mon a feature of Whitechapel, were conspicuous by their absence. Crime made fewer demands upon them than further east. A hansom came jingling towards her; she looked at it longingly, but without money or any clear destination there was no point in hailing it.

Crossing the road, she turned down a small street that led her into a big open space that looked like public gardens. It was Camden Chapel cemetery, an even more unwelcoming spot than usual under a pall of snow. To the south of the Chapel was another large building, which, tramping round to the front of it, she saw was the Foundling Hospital.

'Pity I can't tie meself to the door-handle and get taken in,' she thought. By now her worn boots were sodden, her shoulders, hair and hat thick with melting flakes that trickled down her neck. The snow driving in her face made it difficult for her to see where she was going; once she stumbled and fell over some obstruction on the pavement hidden by the deceptive whiteness. Her head was still aching from her previous fall, and it was becoming obvious that she had bruised her right arm and side.

Tears began to well in her eyes, but, scrambling up, she told herself not to be a fool. You couldn't get lost in the snow in London, like you could in Russia and such places. Not in 1900, anyway. Why, one of the new wonderful motor-cars might come chugging towards her any minute, and a handsome goggled driver get out and wave her courteously into the back seat. 'My pleasure, Madam. Marlborough House, Madam? I believe His Highness is expecting you.'

The unpleasant fact remained that she *was* lost in London. Tracking back along the side of the Foundling, she found herself in a rich-looking square with trees in the middle and tall houses, link-extinguishers on their gateposts. With sudden resolution, she went up the steps of the first one she came to and rang the bell, terrified at the sound it made. The door was answered by a man, in a dark suit. 'Yes?' he said unpromisingly.

'If you please, sir –' she began. The butler raised a pontifical right hand.

'We don't give to beggars here,' he said, and shut the door in her face. Clemence descended the steps and described him in the very worst language she knew. It gave her the impetus to try another imposing front door. This time a middle-aged maid answered, resplendent in her Sunday gown and apron. Clemence began to gabble.

'Please, I know I look like a beggar but I'm not, I've been robbed and I can't find my way and –'

The maid looked her up and down with undisguised scorn.

'Try the police-station,' she said. Before Clemence could get another word out the door was shut, and she heard a chain fastened inside.

A few churchgoers appeared, coming home from evening service on foot or in their own conveyances, the horses' hoofbeats muffled by the snow. She moved towards a house at which a brougham was unloading a family, and stood by the area railings, visible by the light of a street-lamp, hoping that someone would take pity on her. An elderly couple and a young woman got out and went into the house without, it seemed, being aware of her presence. Beggars were ten a penny, and loitering young girls were more often than not prostitutes.

Dejected, she turned away and wandered on, sharply hungry by now and chilled to the bone. There were lights in area-windows where servants were enjoying Sunday evening peace and their supper! Supper! What a beautiful thought. She staggered with weakness, clinging to some spear-headed railings through which the kitchen lights beckoned alluringly like will-o'-the-wisps. Perhaps servants would be kinder than masters. The thought emboldened her to go down the steep area-steps and knock timidly on the door. A fearful outburst of barking from what sounded like a bloodthirsty wolfhound was the response. Trembling she knocked again, with the same result. Then the barks died down, as though somebody had removed the dog or ordered it to stop. The door was unbolted and opened just enough for Clemence to see the face of a woman peering through.

'Be off or I'll set the dog on you. We know your sort!'

159

said the face, and the door was slammed and rebolted. A heady fragrance of cooking had wafted through it, crazing Clemence with hunger. She toiled up the steps again and resumed her weary trudge. A man appeared round a corner, and, seeing her, slowed down. Her heart leapt with hope. He looked neither particularly gentlemanly nor particularly common, just ordinary. She managed to smile at him as he approached her.

'Hello, girlie,' he said. 'How much?'

Without answering she rushed past him and began to run, hearing his voice calling something after her. When she was sure he wasn't following she slowed down to a walking pace. She was in a crescent now, its name obliterated by snow. The tall houses had built-out porches; one, she saw, was partly walled, forming a kind of sentry-box.

All right, she thought, that's it. I give up. At least it won't snow on me in there, and with luck I might last the night. She opened the iron gate cautiously, in case it squeaked and somebody rushed out to investigate. The floor of the porch was of marble, reasonably dry. She crept into the farthest corner of it and sat down, her head leaning against the door-frame, her coat wrapped tightly round her. It was an intense relief to stop walking. Relaxed, she drifted into a state half-thought, half-dream. What would she have for supper, if she could order it? Irish stew, or tripe and onions, toad-in-the-hole, or lots and lots of bacon and eggs with a nice crisp piece of fried bread? And for afters Apple Charlotte or a chocolate custard and an ice-cream and a big pot of strong steaming tea . . .

But her nose was running constantly, the little handkerchief in her pocket was soaking wet, and made her upper lip sore when she used it. There'd been clean hankies in the hat-box. What a good thing she'd given Sophy the little cupid with the hearts and the china dog and Mum's brooch, the only ornaments they had. Funny to think she'd probably never see them again, or ever see Sophy again.

She wondered whether Mum and Dad and Charlie and Sam and Inkerman knew she was dying, and whether they'd come to meet her. She saw them in her mind, lined up along the bank of a river over which she was rowing towards them, in a little boat that suddenly turned itself into Mr. Blackwood's Boat Race winner, with the Broadstairs figurehead cutting through the waves. The noise of the waves was very loud in her head, and then consciousness left her.

When she woke up she was in Heaven, of course. It was gloriously warm and light and smelt of beautiful food. Her sopping clothes were gone, and she was wrapped in something deliciously soft.

'There now, she's coming round!' said a comfortable voice. 'Thank Heaven!'

'Yes, indeed,' said another voice, very sweet and precise and ladylike. 'I think we have saved a life tonight, Mrs. Watts.'

How odd to thank Heaven when you're *in* Heaven, thought Clemence, opening her eyes with an effort. She was quite relieved to see that she was still on Earth, in a room with a cheerful wallpaper and a canary in a cage by the window, a rocking-chair by the fire, and she was lying on a sofa, wrapped in blankets.

The two women who had spoken were a stout middle-aged woman with a pleasant face, dressed in something plain and dark, with a frilled cap on her grey hair, and a tall, elegant lady. One judged her to be a 'lady' rather than a 'woman', instantly. She might have been any age between thirty and fifty. She had the kind of hair which might be very pale blonde or a darker blonde going white, and her face, though it had a mature look, was as pink and white as a girl's, obviously without the aid of cosmetics. Her eyes were a limpid china blue, her expression pleasant to the point of insipidity. She was dressed in something grey and blue, with a high lacy collar, and earrings made like little birds' eggs, blue and spotted, dangled from her ears. Clemence watched them, drowsily, as the lady nodded in satisfaction.

'Dear girl,' she said, 'do you know that you have the most

161

delightful aura? A very light violet, with overtones of silver – quite remarkable.'

As Clemence, even in her normal state, had not the faintest notion what an aura was, she could only smile faintly.

'Yes,' the lady went on, 'with an aura of such quality you were obviously not intended to pass over to the Other Side just yet. We can't spare you here in Earthland, you know!' and she shook a playful finger.

Clemence decided that the lady was mad; how easy it was to escape from a madhouse, if one weren't mad oneself? But perhaps she was, in which case the situation became even more complicated. She shut her eyes again.

'Beef tea, I think, Mrs. Watts,' the high precise voice was saying.

'Or what about a nice chicken broth?' suggested her companion. 'Or there's the calves'-foot jelly we got when you had that bad turn in the summer.' The lady could be heard musing, her voice sending Clemence off into drowsiness. She was awakened by a hand gently shaking her shoulder and looked up to see Mrs. Watts smiling down at her and holding a cup from which came a savoury steam.

'Come along, sit up, there's a good girl,' she said. Clemence obeyed, wondering why her back and limbs felt so stiff. Because she seemed unable to lift her hand Mrs. Watts began to feed her with the broth by spoonfuls. It was the most delicious stuff she had ever tasted in her life. The lady watched, smiling.

CHAPTER THIRTEEN

For some days Clemence was iller than she had ever been. She had a violent cold and cough, fever and racking bone-ache, just missing the dreaded pneumonia which in 1900 was usually fatal. She remembered very little about her illness, except for the awareness that she was in bed in a room with a tent-shaped ceiling like the one at Black Lion Yard. The wallpaper was dazzlingly lovely to Clemence's eyes: thousands of fruits and berries rioted against blue boughs and stems, giving the beholder the sensation of gazing into a great blue tree. It was William Morris's 'Fruit' design, one of his masterpieces.

From wall to wall the floor was carpeted in soft jade-green, patterned with lilies; the furniture was delicate and modern, comfortable chairs of ebony wood with cane seats the colour of new bread. The wardrobe had painted figures on it, and the picture over the white mantelpiece was a scene in which women (or they might be angels) in diaphanous robes, with long fire-red hair, moved in a sort of moonscape of silver cloud and starshine.

As for the bed, it was a revelation to a girl who had slept all her life on hard, narrow old mattresses, sometimes shared with another child. This mattress had springs that made her feel she was being rocked in a little boat on a calm sea, soothing aching limbs and hot skin. Its coverlet was an old-fashioned patchwork quilt, a field of colour and materials for the heavy eyes to explore: stripes and rosebuds, gold thread and velvet, checked gingham and scarlet flannel rivalled and complemented each other.

Clemence was sure she would not have got better so quickly without the room. She said so, when her hostess came to visit her on the fifth day since her arrival. The Lady, as Clemence thought of her, smiled her ethereal smile.

'You are a natural sensitive, child. Did you know that?'

'No, miss,' said Clemence, wide-eyed. 'I don't know what that is.'

'Dear me, what a pity,' the Lady sighed. 'Such a wonderful thing, to be one of Us. Shall I explain it to you – that is, if you feel well enough?'

Clemence did feel well enough. She hauled herself up in bed against the pillows, and the Lady wrapped a soft pink shawl round her shoulders.

'Do you know how I recognised you as a sensitive? When Mrs. Watts found you in the porch and we carried you downstairs, I saw that even in your unconscious state you had a remarkable aura.'

Clemence looked blank.

'An aura, child, is a mystical radiation from the body, sometimes of one colour, sometimes of many. By it we may know the soul. If the aura is dark and murky, oh beware! But if it is like yours, beautiful rays of violet and silver, then the soul within is clear and noble.' She saw Clemence's astonished eyes surveying the area round her own figure.

'No, child, you will not see mine; you are not yet mature in the world of Spirit.'

Light broke on Clemence. 'You're a Spiritualist, aren't you?' The Lady bowed her head.

'They call us so, and we are proud of the name. I myself am a medium, the link between earth and Summerland. You, in time, may become a healer, since you responded so quickly to the vibrations of my Healing Room.' She looked round complacently. 'The blue of sky and the green of Nature, the lilies of purity, the gold of sunshine, all working together to restore the wounded body . . . And now I will tell you your story. Oh yes, I know that you, the waif, should be telling it to me. But I want to prove to you that I have supernormal powers.'

'Go on!' Clemence was intrigued.

'Let me see, now. You are an orphan. Both your parents and another near relation – yes, a child, a brother – are in spirit. You have been held back by circumstances from development both in earthly and spiritual ways. Your blood is not wholly English. I see a dark man – with black curly hair – and behind him a woman in bright dress. She's in a sunny country. Well, well: she is a negress, I see, and she is saying that she handed down her psychic power to you.'

Clemence nodded, awestruck.

'Don't be afraid to tell me if I'm right, child. The spirits thrive on vocal vibrations. What else? There is an ugly room – women sitting on the floor . . . the spirits are showing me a needle and thread. They're sewing – is that it? I thought so. Now a change – a large building with a great deal of red, and bright lights. I see you standing – on a stage!' she exclaimed triumphantly. 'And I tell you something else, child, you'll stand there again. Yes, you've come a long way to reach me – many sorrows . . .' She spoke to an invisible informant. 'I can't hear you, speak up. Boots? They're showing me a pair of broken boots, child, and a symbol of death, crossed out. I think he means that if you had stayed out longer in the snow you would have passed over. And what a pity that would have been! But never mind, here you are, and how happy we're going to be.'

She beamed on the wondering Clemence. 'So you believe me?'

'Oh, *yes*. And all what you said was true. It's wonderful! I was on the stage, and I did work in a sweat-shop – and all the rest of it. And I know I'm – what you said, syke something, because I used to see people who weren't there, and know about things before they happened, and my Mum said it came from my great-grandmother who was black and came from the West Indies.'

'There!' the Lady was triumphant. 'Now we've learned all that matters about you, let me tell you about myself.' Clemence leaned back comfortably. She suspected that the Lady liked to talk at great length; and she was right.

During the next half-hour she learnt that she was in a house in Burton Crescent, Bloomsbury, near the great railway termini of St. Pancras, King's Cross and Euston. The lady, who owned the house (actually owned, not rented!)

was Miss Lydia Pagenell, and a professional Spiritualist medium.

'By professional, child, I mean that when people come to me seeking help or communication with their dear ones I accept a fee from them, except when they are clearly too poor to afford one. My fees vary according to the length of the sitting, the type of communication used, and so forth. And if you ask me why I accept money for work which is concerned with the healing of the soul, I must point out that doctors accept it for healing the body. Without this peaceful house, and the money to keep its vibrations tuneful, I would be of little use to the world.'

It all reminded Clemence of Mr. Blackwood's sermons, and she rather wished Miss Pagenell would get on and demonstrate a bit of her magic (which it clearly was). She'd always been fascinated by that sort of thing, mind-reading and conjuring tricks, and had often watched the same act over and over again when she was working the halls.

But instead of a magic show tea arrived, borne by Mrs. Watts, the pleasant well-spoken woman who had been her rescuer.

'I was so taken aback, Miss Moffat' (she had told them her name) 'you could have knocked me down with a feather. Nine times out of ten, once the front-door's bolted and chained it stays bolted and chained till morning. Now why should I go and open it that night? I think it was to see if the steps wanted sweeping down in case they iced over in the night. But more likely it was a Call. So I opened the door, and there you were, lying like a corpse and as cold as one. Well, I shouted for the girl, that's Annie, from the Foundling, and we got you in, and only just in time.'

It was plain that Mrs. Watts had a great admiration for her employer, and the relationship between them became even clearer when, after another two days in bed, Clemence was able to come downstairs. She was invited to sit in Mrs. Watts's parlour, the room in which she had come to her senses, as a nice compromise between upstairs and downstairs life. As the housekeeper's room, it was furnished comfortably as a sitting-room, in which Mrs. Watts could take her after-meal nap while Cook, who came in by the day, got rid of the debris in the adjoining kitchen. Sitting in the rocking-chair by the fire, her feet on the brass fender, and her lap weighed down with the enormous tabby cat, Thomas, she learned the routine of a typical day in the Pagenell household.

Miss Pagenell would arise, bathe in the hip-bath which stood at the foot of her bed ('the spirits love cleanliness'), then run briskly three times round the back garden, barefoot. At first this had caused comment among the neighbours, who prophesied that one day she would be Come For and Taken Away, but by now they were quite used to her, even if they didn't understand that bodily contact with Mother Earth as near daybreak as possible is an invaluable aid to mediumship.

Then, after a light breakfast, she would retire to her Sanctum, a room furnished in every shade of blue, from palest opal to the dark cerulean of a Mediterranean sea. There were pictures in it like the one of Clemence's bedroom, of strange airy beings with coloured rays around them which she took to be auras; and on the round table, in the centre, stood an object covered with a black velvet cloth, and a curious wooden thing.

Clemence took in all this when she was first shown the Sanctum, and longed to know what went on there. Her notions of Spiritualism were still confused with tame doves and vanishing tricks and Sawing a Lady in Half.

Soon after Miss Pagenell had settled down in the Sanctum, the front door bell would ring and Mrs. Watts would answer it. Why this was not the duty of the maid, Annie, Clemence couldn't make out. Mrs. Watts wasn't exactly any chicken to keep going up and down all those stairs. After an hour or so, sometimes less, the client would be heard departing, usually overlapping with the next one. And so it went on all day. Clemence nearly jumped out of her skin the first time the telephone rang in the hall. She had never heard or seen one before, and was inclined to class it with Spiritualism and conjuring.

All day Clemence stayed in the housekeeper's room, listening to the comings and goings above, idling through a few books that had pictures in them, and providing a warmed resting-place for Thomas. What was she doing here, she wondered? Miss Pagenell was obviously well off, and could afford to keep her for a bit, but why should she? She looked down at her dress, washed and beautifully pressed like the rest of her clothes, but beyond all question too shabby for Burton Crescent. Annie obviously regarded her with suspicion, peering through the glass panes of the door that separated kitchen and parlour as though she expected Clemence to be stuffing her pockets with spoons.

'Thinks there's something fishy going on,' she reflected. 'Shouldn't wonder if there is.'

She had been rescued once before, and got into an impossible situation as a result. Was this rescue operation going to lead to something of the same kind? You got so suspicious of people when you had an experience like that.

And yet Mrs. Watts, when she came down to wait with Clemence in the evening, was the soul of ordinariness and respectability. Knitting steadily, she talked of the war in South Africa, of her girlhood in Bristol, of the Queen's Diamond Jubilee three years before and of the probability of Her Majesty living to see another Jubilee in 1907. On and on went her level voice, punctuated by the sleepy twitter of of her canary in its cage by the window, and the gentle snoring of Thomas in Clemence's lap. Clemence's head nodded forward.

'Well, I never, Miss Moffat, you're ready for your bed, I can see that.' Efficiently she was taken upstairs to her beautiful room, and fell asleep instantly in its soothing atmosphere.

　　　§　　　§　　　§　　　§　　　§

After supper on the following evening Miss Pagenell summoned her upstairs. One of the bells of graded sizes above

Mrs. Watts's door tinkled; 'That's the drawing-room,' said the housekeeper. 'Miss Pagenell would like you to go up.'

How did she know, Clemence wondered?

Miss Pagenell was waiting for her in the pretty drawing-room, which was much more like a room in an ordinary house than the Sanctum. She welcomed Clemence graciously, remarking on her improved looks and asking how she had passed the time. Clemence sensed that these were the preliminaries to something else, and her heart began to beat faster, with memories of the last private interview she had had in Bancroft Street.

'My dear Miss Moffat,' said Miss Pagenell affably at last, 'I can read your thoughts well enough to know that you are afraid I am going to ask of you something you would rather not do.'

Clemence jumped. 'Yes, I was, but –'

'I will tell you what it is, and if it is not agreeable to you you will be perfectly free to say so, and to find yourself a respectable situation.

'I'm going to confide a little secret to you, my child. You are impressed with my psychic powers, I know. And with reason.' Complacently she smoothed the skin of her long white hands, bare of rings. 'At my best I am very good. But I am not always at my best. Tell me, how old do you think I am?'

Blushing with embarrassment, Clemence studied the porcelain complexion, the silver-gilt hair. No wrinkles, no lines. And yet there was something . . .

'Thirty?' she guessed.

An enigmatic smile and a slow shake of the head.

'Add thirty years and you'll be near the mark.'

Clemence's mouth fell open with astonishment.

'You see, child, a life of communion with the spirits and High Forces for Good keeps the body young and relaxed. There are no tensions, no worries. All will be solved by Spirit.'

'And yet,' she leaned forward earnestly, 'the body grows tired as it ages, in such strenuous work as mine. With every client a little more power goes out of me. By teatime I am drained, my life-force is almost spent.' One pale hand drifted across her marble brow. 'And so, when I can no longer see into the mind of my sitter, or call up the spirits to interpret, I resort to other means.'

She fixed Clemence with a piercing blue gaze. 'A very little knowledge of psychology, a few questions, discreetly asked, and any one of us can learn all we need to know of another person. Do you understand me?'

'I – think so.'

'I am going to ask you if you, with your undeveloped powers, will help in this. For a consideration and your board, of course.'

Clemence was half-attracted, half-repelled. On the one hand it would be exciting to work in this realm of mystery, thrilling to find out people's secrets; and on the other the word Fishy rang insistently in her ears. 'But beggars can't be choosers,' she reminded herself. 'No more Missions for me, nor sweat-shops either, and it's that or slaving up and down with hot water and coal-buckets like that Annie.' Aloud she said 'I'd like to try.'

Miss Pagenell beamed on her. 'How very wise of you, and how glad you will be one day that you trained under a medium of my quality. Sir Oliver Lodge, Sir William Crooks, Mr. Myers, Doctor Stainton Moses – I have sat with them all. The great age of mediumship is dawning, my child, with this new century, and you shall be its prophet.'

It was agreed that on Monday (no clients were seen on Sunday) Clemence should attend two sittings, to observe Miss Pagenell's mediumship under different conditions. On the Sunday night she hardly slept. People seemed to be all round her, voices speaking and laughing in her ears, visions in colours unearthly bright forming and dissolving behind her closed eyelids, snatches of music played. She woke feeling as if she had been on a long, long journey. At nine o'clock, half an hour before the first client was due, she presented herself in the Sanctum. Miss Pagenell, elegant in turquoise, was in position at the round table. She beckoned.

She picked up the little wooden thing shaped like a painter's pallet, with a pencil stuck through it, supporting it like a leg.

'This is my ouija board or planchette. Under a light pressure it will write messages and answers dictated by the spirits. And this,' whisking off the black velvet cloth, 'is my crystal.'

Clemence had heard of the crystal ball used by fortune-tellers at fairs and the seaside, and had imagined it to be a large object scintillating like cut glass. To her disappointment it was hardly bigger than a cricket ball, balanced on an ebony base, and seemed opaque.

'Can you really see things in it?' she asked.

'The crystal is not a miniature kinematograph, child. A mature medium does not rely on it, she uses it merely as a focal point.'

'You mean like when you look at a bright light your eyes get fixed, and you can't look away?'

'Something like that. Tealeaves serve the same purpose.'

'Oh, yes!' Clemence cried eagerly. 'I can do those. It isn't that you really see pictures in them – you see what the shapes *mean*.'

'Exactly. And now I want you to sit behind this screen.' She led Clemence to a corner where stood a tall screen, decorated with a painting of a rural landscape, a castle in the background. A chair was behind it, on which Clemence was to sit; through the wide division between two of the screen's sections it was possible to see anything that happened at the table.

'Remember, you must be very quiet. My sitter's confidence would be shaken if she knew she was overheard.'

The bell rang. Miss Pagenell composed herself at the table, her elbows resting on it and the fingers lightly clasped. The door opened, and to Clemence's surprise Mrs. Watts entered.

'The Honourable Emily Cartwright,' she said, quietly. Then, loudly, 'Mrs. Winter.'

A murmur of voices as Mrs. Watts showed the sitter in. Clemence saw a woman of about thirty-eight, elegantly dressed, a feather boa flung round her neck, her hat a fruit-crammed creation like a miniature Harvest Festival. She looked pale, and when she sat in the chair opposite Miss Pagenell her gloved hands were twisting nervously.

'Good morning, Mrs. Winter,' said Miss Pagenell cordially. Behind the screen Clemence was startled. Why had Mrs. Watts announced the visitor by another name?

'Shall we begin with a little prayer?' the medium went on. Mrs. Winter, or whatever her real name was, murmured acquiescence and bowed her head while Miss Pagenell recited a short request to the Great Spirit to preside over the sitting.

'And now,' sitting up briskly, 'let us see how Myra and I can help you. Myra is my guide, a dear little girl who passed to the Summerland at the age of seven, fifty years or so ago. You may not hear her voice, Mrs. Winter, but she would be very pleased if you would speak to her.'

Mrs. Winter looked startled and embarrassed. 'What – what shall I say?'

'Anything you like.'

Mrs. Winter gulped, and said stiffly, 'Good morning, Myra.'

From somewhere came a little piping voice. 'Good morning, nice lady.' Then Miss Pagenell's.

'There! She spoke to you; she doesn't often do that. You must be an excellent subject.'

The sitter smiled faintly, and said, 'May I ask you things?'

'No need at all. Myra knows what is in your mind and will do her best to help you. Myra, dear!' She paused for a moment and appeared to be listening. 'Yes. Is she? Clever girl. I'll tell her.' She turned to the woman.

'Myra tells me, Mrs. Winter, that you have some great trouble on your mind. Not a bereavement, she thinks. (Yes, Myra? Very well.) Someone is standing beside Myra, she says, some connection of yours. A small lady. Oldish. She seems to be carrying something; could it be a stick, with a whitish handle? Yes, of course. Ivory. She's showing it to

172

me. There's something else. An animal. Oh, it's a little brown dog. Do you recognise her?'

For the first time Mrs. Winter's face was animated.

'My grandmamma!' she exclaimed. 'She always walked with her ivory stick because of her rheumatism. And the little dog is Pepino. She was so fond of him. How wonderful!'

Miss Pagenell was listening again. 'She sends you her love and – just a moment, there's a message . . . Yes, I've got it. The ring. Remember the ring. What? I didn't catch – oh yes. She's saying "Blest be the tie that binds." Does that mean anything?'

The sitter's eyes had stolen to her gloved left hand. Her eyes were glistening with tears. Her 'Yes' was barely audible.

'Now there's someone else coming. A soldier, yes.' Mrs. Winter's face was glowing with excitement. Or was it fear?

Myra's voice piped up. 'Emmy! darling Emmy!' Then Miss Pagenell asked, 'Have you a father in spirit?'

Mrs. Winter leaned forward eagerly. 'Yes! He always called me Emmy. My name is Emily. Papa, oh papa! May I speak to him?' The medium shook her head.

'He's gone now, I'm afraid. He passed over some time ago, and is far from this world. But he will be with you if you call him, in time of trouble.' Clemence noticed that Miss Pagenell's voice was becoming slower, almost slurred; her head was tipped back, resting against her chair. Now she spoke quite differently, in a monotone. 'There's another soldier. On earth. He says he will come back. Something more. Lady? Lady? I can't catch. Lady – Smith? He's smiling. He says dearest – love. Dearest love.' Her voice dropped away. Mrs. Winter was crying, her hands clasped imploringly, talking to the unseen spirit.

'Hugh, Hugh darling! Oh, please come back! Hugh, I've done something – terrible – while you've been away. I was afraid, so afraid, you'd be killed – so far from me – as my punishment. Oh, darling, if you'll only come back, I'll never do such a thing again. Forgive, please forgive!' Miss Pagenell's slow voice interrupted.

'He is in this world. But he is asleep; it is his astral that

173

speaks to you, his other self that journeys where it wishes while he sleeps. He says he has been ill, but not seriously. He points to something coloured – a medal. He says you will be proud . . . proud . . .' The voice faded. Miss Pagenell sat up and passed a hand across her eyes as though sweeping off a veil.

'Did I say something useful?' she asked the sitter, who was still weeping. She pulled herself together.

'Yes, yes. Thank you a thousand times. You don't know what you've done for me.'

'I'm afraid there's nothing else I can tell you – the power has gone.'

'No, no, please don't worry. I've heard all I need.' She rose and opened her handbag. 'I don't like to talk about money – but what you've said this morning was worth the whole world to me. May I –?'

Miss Pagenell smiled deprecatingly. 'If you would give me two pounds I shall consider myself well rewarded. A percentage of what my sitters give me goes to charity.'

With cordial farewells, they parted, and the sitter, transformed and radiant, left the Sanctum.

'You can come out now, Miss Moffat,' the medium called. Clemence emerged.

'Well? What did you think of that?'

Clemence hesitated. 'I thought it was very interesting, but –'

'But what?'

'I hope you won't be angry – but I didn't think Myra was real.'

Miss Pagenell laughed. 'Very good! And what part of it did you think was real?'

'The part when you put your head back and talked slowly. I thought that was ever so shivery.'

Miss Pagenell patted her arm approvingly. 'Absolutely right. At that moment I was in a trance, and I have no idea what I said; one never remembers. The rest of the information was gathered from other sources.'

Clemence was puzzled. 'How?'

174

'The Honourable Emily Cartwright was unwise enough to call at the house to make an appointment for herself, using the name of Winter. But my Mrs. Watts is an avid reader of magazines featuring High Society, and recognised the lady. Then, knowing that she lived in Bloomsbury, Mrs. Watts did some shopping in the district. Shopkeepers, and particularly post-mistresses, can be very informative about ladies with titles; from them Mrs. Watts learned that the graves of Mrs. Cartwright's grandmother and father were in the local churchyard, and her grandmother was described: a little old lady leaning on an ivory-handled stick, with her favourite poodle. As for Mrs. Cartwright's "trouble" she was well known to have – shall we say entertained – a certain noble lord during the husband's absence in South Africa.'

Clemence's face was a study in astonishment. 'I'd never have believed it!' she said.

'This afternoon you shall learn some more methods of drawing out information from clients,' said Miss Pagenell.

And so she did. The sitter, an elderly woman, was obviously bereaved, being in black from head to foot. Miss Pagenell deduced simply enough that she had not lost a husband, for she wore no ring; or a parent, for she was too old. A selection of common names, which the sitter racked her memory to recognise, produced finally a Martha for whom she was wearing mourning. 'Martha' sent comforting if predictable messages, saying that she was happy in a beautiful place full of flowers, that one day she and her sister would meet again, and that she had met Mama. The sitter departed, overwhelming Miss Pagenell with thanks and willingly parting with two pounds.

'Now,' said Miss Pagenell to Clemence, 'you see how I work. Will you help me, and help Mrs. Watts, by making a few enquiries for me now and then? You will be paid, of course.' Clemence had already decided.

'Yes, I will; it seems funny, deceiving people, but I can see it does 'em a lot of good, the more you can say. But I don't understand what you said when you didn't remember this morning. Who was Lady Smith? Mrs. Cartwright didn't say anything about her.' ·

Miss Pagenell shook her head, smiling. 'Wait, wait, and you will understand.'

The next day, February 28, the besieged township of Ladysmith was relieved by British forces under General Buller.

☰   ☰   ☰   ☰   ☰

Clemence's status did not remain quite so grand as when she joined the household. She was soon removed from the Healing Room (which, she discovered, was often let to ailing clients) and transferred to a plain small bedroom. Miss Pagenell made it quite clear, very tactfully, that Clemence was expected to earn her keep by doing a good many jobs which took the weight off Mrs. Watts's legs. These included acting as personal maid to Mrs. Pagenell, which Clemence enjoyed, on the whole.

No longer did she share the drawing-room in the evenings. Mrs. Watts, the cat Thomas and sulky Alice were her leisure company, and though her powers of mimicry increased, her accents and manners remained, regrettably, the same.

Ah well, she thought; it's all Life. And even in a Spiritualist household you never know what Fate's going to send you.

CHAPTER FOURTEEN

It was Fate that Stephen came along when he did. For three
and a half years, or rather more, Clemence worked happily
as Miss Pagenell's assistant. She learnt as much about ordinary people as about mediumship. There were sitters who
came along willing you to say what they wanted to hear,
even pretending that they recognised the name of Maud or
William, so that you would get on to something they really
did recognise. Others were grimly sceptical, defying you to
convince them. Some were manifestly shattered by the loss
of a dear one, harrowing your feelings with their grief; others
worldly and self-seeking, wanting to know where Auntie had
hidden her will, the old wretch, before she died.

And of course there were the women who wanted Miss
Pagenell to make them up love-potions, or put a curse on
somebody, both of which she politely declined to do, though
charging them a nominal fee for her advice, which sometimes led to a full sitting. And there were the bored people,
usually rich, who made a habit of consulting mediums out
of curiosity and as a change from Bridge. They were the
least interesting clients.

Just occasionally, Miss Pagenell would be persuaded to
give a demonstration of physical mediumship and Direct
Voice. This meant that members of her private Circle, with
any friends who were not professional 'ghost-hunters' or
police, would meet at her house. When the company was
assembled in the Sanctum and the time seemed propitious,
the lights were extinguished and one lamp left burning, with
a blue shade over it.

With a majestic step, Miss Pagenell would enter the
medium's 'cabinet', a tent-like affair of canvas rigged on
wood supports ('like a clothes-horse,' Clemence thought).
When she was inside and seated on a small chair two members of the Circle would ritually bind her hands and feet so

that no trickery was possible. Then they would resume their places, touching hands and singing to encourage the psychic energy to flow. Individual taste dictated a surprising range of song, from *Rock of Ages* and *Abide with Me* to *John Brown's Body* and (once only) *Nellie Dean*. The trouble with this was that Clemence, the indispensable ally behind the scenes, almost choked herself with laughter every time the company began its solemn, earnest chant. At first she used to bury her face in the folds of a curtain, but this was inclined to make her sneeze. Miss Pagenell had to speak to her sharply before she learnt to control herself.

Once the singing had stopped the manifestations began. What wonders were seen! A luminous trumpet appeared, floating about the room, voices of different kinds issuing from it with messages for this or that person. Sometimes it was accompanied by a tambourine, also luminous. Ladies would find a flower laid in the lap by unseen hands, or a cheap ornament or semi-precious stone; a light kiss would touch the back of a hand. A clean handkerchief, provided by one of the Circle, did the most surprising things, including forming itself into a glove-shape, and sliding along the floor like a snake, to disappear under a curtain. But the moment everybody waited for was when the 'apparitions' came out of the cabinet.

One by one, with intervals between, they appeared, of various shapes and sizes, but quite obviously not Miss Pagenell, who could be heard breathing heavily in trance. A child, a bent old woman, a young man with dark moustache and hair, came in turn, and were immediately recognised as their dear departed by one Circle member or another. It was quite remarkable, Clemence thought, considering that they were all her. Miss Pagenell had learnt something from Miss Florence Cook, materialisation medium of Sir William Crookes, who for his delight had produced 'Katie King', an apparition claiming to be a relation of the seventeenth-century pirate, Henry Morgan. Clemence would love to have impersonated a lady pirate, but no such lively role came her way.

The years passed like lightning: she was nineteen, twenty, and in 1903 twenty-one. Queen Victoria had died, and pleasure-loving Edward VII was king. Aristocratic England devoted its time to such popular sports as duck-shooting and adultery. Sir Arthur Conan Doyle, who would be a Spiritualist leader in a few years, brought the supposedly dead Sherlock Holmes back to life with *The Hound of the Baskervilles*. The Wright brothers made the first flight of Man in a heavier-than-air machine, Henry Ford was busy inventing a motor-car which would not break down five minutes from home, stopping the traffic and frightening the horses.

And Clemence lived on in the calm house where so many amazing things took place, seeing Sophy marry a reassuringly steady young man, Thomas departing his life to be replaced by a ginger kitten, Miss Pagenell's Pre-Raphaelite beauty begin to fade. She was very tired.

'For all her little tricks she works like a donkey, and good luck to her!' Clemence said to Mrs. Watts, who was now her firm friend, relieved that she had taken over so much of the work and brought them many clients.

There was a sad day in the summer of 1903 when Miss Pagenell appeared to them in the downstairs parlour, white-faced beneath her delicate touch of rouge. The front door had just slammed with violence.

'I couldn't see anything for him!' she cried. 'He wouldn't help me, recognise a single name or give me a clue. He says he's going to report me to the police for fraud!' She collapsed on the sofa, and was comforted by Clemence and Mrs. Watts.

'Of course he won't! Any medium's bound to have an off-day.'

She gave them a watery smile, and thanked them, before trailing wearily back to the Sanctum.

'But I don't like it, I don't like it a bit,' Mrs. Watts said. 'You're a smart girl, Clemence, but one of these days you'll get caught if she doesn't. Oh, drat that kitten, he'll have to live in the coalhouse if he won't learn clean habits.'

It was the most golden August day of that golden Edwardian summer when Stephen came to Burton Crescent. To Clemence's eyes, dazzled by the sun where she sat in the garden, he was golden too. His crisp curly hair caught the sun and made a halo, and light glittered on the gold down on the back of his hand, as he raised his hat to her. She gave him her warmest smile. Gentleman clients, young ones, at least, were as rare as snowdrops in July. She watched him enter the house with enjoyment.

When he came out again half an hour later his face wore a strained, disappointed look. Something impelled Clemence to give him a smile which this time was frankly come-hither, or chase-me-Charlie.

'Isn't it hot,' she said. 'Got far to go?'

'Good afternoon.' (He was nothing if not punctilious.) 'Not really far – just back to the Temple.'

'Oh. I thought you might like some tea. I'm having mine out here.'

His face was less tense already. 'I'd like that, very much. How kind of you, Miss – er –'

'Moffat. I'm Miss Pagenell's assistant.'

He looked at her with an interest that was not merely admiration.

'Really! I – I should so much like a word with you.'

'Rightyo.' She had darted round the side of the house to give Annie instructions. Back by his side, she invited him to take the other garden-chair. They surveyed one another covertly. The spark of attraction had been lit and was burning steadily on its way to the powder magazine. They chatted idle of the news, of what they thought about the Votes for Women campaign ('I'm all for it,' Clemence declared) of the new opera *Merrie England*. The tea arrived, with some cakes and ripe strawberries; he said it was just like a garden party, with which she agreed, never having been near one in her life.

Then, putting down his teacup, he turned to her.

'May I ask you something? I hope it isn't a breach of confidence for you to tell me.'

'Fire away, and we'll see.'

His story was on the lines Clemence expected. He was a lawyer, twenty-seven years old, already set up in modest chambers in the Temple. His beloved mother had died three years ago, and he was most anxious to get in touch with her. 'But I'm sorry to say that Miss Pagenell got nowhere near. Not one solitary piece of evidence did she give me; I even caught her trying to get information out of me.'

Clemence tut-tutted.

'I'm really most disappointed. She was recommended to me by a very reliable friend.'

'I think I know the reason,' Clemence said. 'Miss Pagenell hasn't been at all well this summer (the heat, you know) and when she's low her mediumship suffers. Stands to reason. She's wonderful usually; I'm sorry you found her like this.'

He looked relieved. 'Oh! I'm sorry. The layman doesn't take such things into consideration. I was thinking of going to someone else, but . . .'

'Oh, don't do that!' she cut in hastily. 'Why don't you make another appointment, and she'll take care to be really rested that day – for the sake of her reputation, you know!'

He thought that a brilliant idea, and would telephone when he had looked at his engagement diary. They parted, their hands lingering in the farewell clasp. He wanted to come back as much as she wanted to see him again.

Miss Pagenell was not pleased. Upset by a deplorably unsuccessful sitting, she was angry with Clemence for not getting on-the-spot information. 'You could easily have found out where he lived, what his mother's name was, anything. And instead you let him go, you silly girl.'

'I didn't think,' said Clemence meekly.

'Well, you may do some thinking now. You have his name, Stephen Reynolds, and his address. Go down to Fleet Street tomorrow and come back with some solid facts, please!'

Clemence protested at being sent into town on a hot day, and hoped the idea would have been dropped by morning. But it was Miss Pagenell's first instruction to her.

'No Sanctum work today. Off you go.'

So off she went, in a charming muslin dress with a little black velvet band round her throat and the most fetching of straw sailor hats. It was very unfortunate – and yet in another way most fortunate – that she had barely got off the omnibus in the Strand than she ran into Stephen himself.

She went a bright pink; Stephen, who had thought her a pretty girl the day before, now thought her an absolute stunner. There was nothing for it but that they must walk along the Temple together. She made up a hurried tale about having to go to Charing Cross to see about a parcel, to explain her presence.

It was a beautiful morning. Too beautiful to go in. They sat on a seat in Fountain Court, watching the diamond drops of the fountain cascade into the air, making it deliciously cool. He picked a pink rose for her, first looking round in melodramatic pantomime to make sure he was not watched from the windows. She laughed, and blushed again, and put the rose in her blouse, fastening it through a button-hole. How gallant he was, yet shy and even little-boyish at moments; and he had, now and then, a strange look of her father.

An hour had fled by when she remembered her mission. With difficulty and reluctance she found out some of the facts Miss Pagenell wanted. He had been born in Hertford, his mother's name had been Charlotte, his politics were Liberal. It was impossible to bring up the question of the problem.

'I looked in my diary last night,' he said, 'and so far as I know next Wednesday I'm free all afternoon. Would that do for another sitting, do you think?'

'Should think so. If not, can I telephone you?'

'Of course. What a wonderful thing the telephone is!'

'*Isn't* it just!' (and aren't you just, she was thinking).

'Can –' he gave his characteristic little nervous cough – 'can I see you before that? Could you come out on Sunday – or Saturday?'

She could and she would, and they boated on the Serpentine in the afternoon, and went to a foreign restaurant for a meal in the evening. The following Wednesday Stephen came to consult Miss Pagenell again, this time with more satisfactory results; he was too innocent to connect any information he'd given Clemence with what the medium told him. After that he and Clemence met at least once a week, going to the theatre or up river to Richmond by steamer, for cake teas at the Maids of Honour, or to lovely Kew Gardens. Clemence was head over heels in love, and she suspected that he was. Why didn't he *speak*, the sweet silly thing? Perhaps it was the difference in their class. But what did that matter, when they got on so well? He didn't seem to notice the flavour of Whitechapel in her voice, he never corrected her grammar or told her to hold her knife and fork properly.

At the end of September the telephone gave its jarring ring as Clemence was passing through the hall. To her surprise and joy it was Stephen, wanting to make an appointment with Miss Pagenell; after which he would take Clemence out.

A few days later he arrived. Clemence opened the door to him, and lifted her face for the expected kiss. But it did not come, he only pressed her hand and said he would see her later. She felt trouble in the air.

He was with Miss Pagenell over an hour. When he came out his face was set in worry-lines. He hardly seemed to notice her new red coat, worn for the first time. Out in the Crescent he took her arm and they walked slowly over a carpet of fallen leaves towards Euston Road, where Stephen hailed a cab.

'Where to, guv'nor?'

'Oh – anywhere. Regent's Park, and drive round until I stop you.'

The cabbie grinned; he took up a lot of fares who wanted him to drive round and round the Park.

When the cab had started he took her hand and tried to say something. She helped him out.

'Something wrong, isn't it?'

'Yes. I don't know how to tell you, Clemence. But – all

183

the time I've known you, I've been engaged to someone else.'

The shock hit Clemence like a bucket of icy water. 'It's not true,' she said.

'I'm afraid it is, darling. She's a girl who – well, I've known her nearly all my life. That's why I asked her to marry me, I suppose – because I was too shy with other girls.'

Clemence stared unseeingly out of the window. 'Why are you telling me now?'

'Because I've made up my mind that I can't go on with it. At least, I don't *want* to go on with it. You know that. I wanted someone to help me, some advice I could really trust.'

'So – ?'

'So I asked Miss Pagenell to try to contact my mother for me. I knew she'd give me the very best advice.'

Clemence was taut with fear, her hands were clammy and cold. 'And did she succeed?'

'Yes. She couldn't summon my mother's actual voice, but the little guide, Myra, you know, talked for quite a time and said that Mother was strongly against my breaking my promise to the girl she chose for me. She said I was to break any other ties and marry Gertrude as soon as possible.'

'Oh, Stephen. Oh, Stephen!'

He put his arm round her. 'I know it's bad, darling, but –'

She flung away from him. 'It's not that! You don't understand. What she told you wasn't true. It wasn't your mother, and Myra's all a fake. You've been cheated. Oh! I'll never forgive her, never!'

'I don't know what you mean,' he said, white-faced.

'Oh, can't you *see*? Miss Pagenell doesn't want me to marry you. I'm too useful to her, she'd not be able to carry on without me. She has got real powers, you know, but they're failing – I think she's very ill. She could see that you and I were – were in love, and she found the ideal way to stop it. Oh, why didn't you tell me first?'

He didn't answer. The cab had entered Regent's Park by the York Gate, and took its leisurely way along York Terrace and the Outer Circle. Then Stephen said in a voice she'd never heard before, 'You mean that you have helped her to cheat, not only me, but others?'

'Yes. Well, I had to! It wasn't wicked, really; she helps so many people.'

'I suppose you gave her information about me?'

'Yes,' she said miserably.

Stephen leaned out and told the driver to stop. He got out and produced a sovereign. 'Please drive this young lady to wherever she wants to go. Keep the change. I've remembered an appointment.'

'Stephen, wait!' she shrieked at him. His face was set and cold.

'I have some thinking to do, Clemence. I'd rather not see you until I've thought things out.' He raised his hat and walked swiftly away.

But he never did see her again, for the next morning Miss Pagenell had a visitor. The policeman insisted on seeing her personally, despite Mrs. Watts's protests, pushed his way into the Sanctum and delivered a piece of paper to her.

'Information has been laid this day, October 1st, 1903, by William Jacquard, broker, that you the said Lydia Pagenell on the eighth day of July at the above dwelling did profess to tell fortunes to deceive and impose upon certain of His Majesty's subjects . . .'

A similar document was delivered to Clemence. They were summoned to appear before a magistrate, and condemned under the Vagrancy Act of 1824; Miss Pagenell to three months' imprisonment, Clemence to one month. The short-tempered gentleman who had threatened the medium with exposure in July had been goaded by some incident quite unconnected with her to expose her at last, and Clemence with her on information received. Together they were taken off in a police van to the all-female prison, Holloway.

Clemence came out on November 1st. Miss Pagenell never came out, for her failing health had collapsed under the disgrace and hardship of imprisonment; after three weeks she died in the prison infirmary.

185

It seemed strange to be free. When Clemence left Holloway she was given a little money and the clothes she had brought in were given back to her. Apart from them she had nothing. She walked some way along the Camden Road, so that the driver whose cab she hailed wouldn't know she was an ex-prisoner.

But he did. They all had a sort of grey look about them.

She told him to drive to Burton Crescent. It was a wild, cold day, the last of the dry leaves scurrying about, whirling into drifts and eddies. She stood looking up at the house she had left a month before. It was locked and shuttered. When she went next door to ask what had happened, the servant gave her an odd look and seemed reluctant to supply information. But Clemence gathered that immediately after Miss Pagenell's death a cousin of hers to whom she had left all her property had come and locked everything up until something called Probate was settled.

'Mrs. Watts? what happened to her?'

The servant sniffed. 'Dismissed, I expect. She never said nothing to me, but I saw that Annie crying and carrying on. They say the house'll be sold, and good riddance, I say. Next time perhaps we'll have respectable people next door.'

Clemence thanked her and turned away. She had exactly nothing in the world except a carpet-bag, the cupid and the crucifix in Sophy's care, the china dog her father had given her, and her remaining money, one pound twelve and sixpence. Where could she go? Not to Stephen, for she sensed that he could never forgive her. Not to Sophy, who was living with her husband in one room. 'Need time to think, you do,' she told herself, walking away from the empty blank-eyed house.

Near Euston Station she saw several houses with notices in their windows which she knew said ROOMS TO LET. She picked a fairly clean-looking one, told the landlady airily that her bags were in the Left Luggage at the station, and gave her the china dog and the bag to hold as hostage, in case, the landlady darkly said, she took it into her head to do a moonlight.

She spent the next morning sitting on a platform on Euston Station, watching the trains go in and out. It was a good place for thinking, and you could get food without leaving the station. She had her first good meal for a month, and, to her relief, began to feel like herself again.

So what should she do now? Only one thing presented itself, though she didn't like to face it. There was always work for a girl in domestic service, however demeaning it might be to one who saw herself as Somebody. She thought back to the little slavey Sue, whom she just remembered, sent back to the orphanage when the Moffats couldn't afford to keep her. She thought of Annie, always bad-tempered and put upon, with a dirty face and hands permanently blackened with coal or reddened with scrubbing. Then she sat up very straight and admonished herself.

'But you're not like them, you're going somewhere. You're Somebody already, in a way. Like Dad used to say, there's always something better round the corner. Come on, Clem, stick your chin out and take a chance on it!'

All very well talking; but how was she to go about it? The answer was literally round the corner. A large policeman loomed up before her and surveyed her sternly.

'Now, young woman,' he said, 'I've been observing you for some time, and it's my opinion you're loitering with intent. If you'll take my advice, you'll move on smartish.'

Clemence gave him a limpid, innocent smile. 'I'm sorry, officer, I didn't think. It's just that I've got nowhere to go. I've lost me job and I don't know where to look for another one.'

'And what kind of job might that be?'

'A place in service, sir, that's what I'm used to,' said Clemence mendaciously. 'Lady's maid, something like that.'

The policeman meditated. 'A domestic agency, that's what you want. Nearest one's Pratt's, just by King's Cross.'

Clemence gave a touching impersonation of a kitten rescued from drowning. 'Oh, *thank* you, officer, ever so much. Which way is it?'

'Turn left outside the station and keep going. And don't

let me see you back here, mind.' He watched the trim figure out of sight, shaking his head. Another one going to the bad, he reckoned.

Pratt's proved to be a small, seedy-looking establishment with a window full of fly-blown, yellowing cards. Clemence went in, heralded by the shrilling of a bell as the door opened and shut. Behind a counter was seated a middle-aged woman with pince-nez perching on a long nose, and an expression of extreme severity. She continued to write in a ledger until Clemence had stood before her for all of a minute, before condescending to raise her head.

'Well, what's your business?'

'I'm looking for a place in service.'

The woman looked her up and down. 'What kind of place?'

'Lady's maid, that's what I've been used to.'

A vinegary smile touched the other's countenance. 'You'd be lucky to get any such thing. What references have you got?'

Clemence had to admit that she had none, much to the satisfaction of Mrs. Bennett. This was exactly the kind of applicant she liked. With satisfaction, she explained that no person could possibly expect to be taken on without references.

'That's that, then.' Clemence turned to leave.

'Not so fast, young woman. Something might be arranged. For a small charge.'

Clemence looked crestfallen. 'How much?'

'Half a crown each.'

Her precious money! Oh, well – it was that or nothing.

'I'll have two.' She laid five shillings on the counter, from which they were swiftly transferred to a drawer. Mrs. Bennett went to an office folder, riffled through it, and handed two rather well-worn sheets of paper to Clemence, who scanned them with what she hoped was an intelligent expression and handed them back.

'One,' said Mrs. Bennett, 'from a lady now gone abroad. The other from an employer now dead. Full name, please.'

188

She wrote it down, together with Clemence's age. As the 'references' were supplied by herself there was no difficulty in matching the handwriting. Then she sorted through a pile of cards. 'Belgrave Square. Cook. Can you cook?'

'Not very well.'

'Charles Street, Mayfair. No, that's gone. Eaton Place, Belgravia. House-parlourmaid. Try that. Come back if not suitable. Good afternoon.'

Clemence, out on the pavement, wondered where one got an omnibus for the address she had in her carpet-bag together with the precious, if dubious, references. She hummed a fragment of one of her old songs, *I went for a ride on a Homnibus, a number seventeen.* She felt fine. After four weeks in Holloway even the air of King's Cross was like a breath of the country; her cheeks were glowing again, after their prison pallor. She took out a cracked piece of mirror one of the other prisoners had given her; yes, she looked as good as ever, and even if she started off as a skivvy it might lead to better things.

'The hell with omnibuses!' she said aloud, to the horror of a passing old lady, and marched briskly to a cab standing on the station rank.

'Where to, miss?'

'Belgravia?' she said grandly, adding in an execrable pidgin-French accent, 'I do not read ze English well. Drive me to zis address,' and she pushed the scribbled-on envelope to the surprised driver. A rum-'un, he thought, but it takes all sorts. 'Righto, Mamzell,' and with a flick of the whip the cab was on its way westwards. Clemence leaned back in her seat and waved regally to imaginary crowds, as she had seen the beautiful Queen Alexandra acknowledge the homage of her people.

Half-an-hour later, outwardly cool and cocky, inwardly taut and nervous with excitement, Clemence was ringing the front-door bell of 165 Eaton Place. Soon she would be Clemence no more. On the other side of the area door, to which Mr. Hudson the butler would very properly direct her, she would be transformed into Sarah.

The 'Upstairs, Downstairs' Series

Here is the full story of the Bellamy family and of their servants from the early days of the twentieth century to the darker age of the First World War.

All are based on the internationally popular series of television plays starring David Langton as Mr. Bellamy and Jean Marsh as Rose.

A selection of General Fiction available from Sphere Books

A selection of Bestsellers from Sphere Books

SARGASSO	Edwin Corley	95p	☐
RAISE THE TITANIC!	Clive Cussler	95p	☐
STORY OF MY LIFE	Moshe Dayan	£1.50p	☐
THE CRASH OF '79	Paul Erdman	£1.25p	☐
EMMA AND I	Sheila Hocken	85p	☐
UNTIL THE COLOURS FADE	Tim Jeal	£1.50p	☐
MAJESTY	Robert Lacey	£1.95p	☐
STAR WARS	George Lucas	95p	☐
KRAMER'S WAR	Derek Robinson	£1.25p	☐
THE GOLDEN SOVEREIGNS	Jocelyn Carew	£1.25p	☐
THE INVASION OF THE BODY SNATCHERS			
	Jack Finney	85p	☐
GOLD FROM CRETE	C. S. Forester	95p	☐
THE GOVERNANCE OF BRITAIN	Harold Wilson	£1.50p	☐
MIDNIGHT EXPRESS			
	Billy Hayes with William Hoffer	95p	☐
CLOSE ENCOUNTERS OF THE THIRD KIND			
	Steven Spielberg	85p	☐
STAR FIRE	Ingo Swann	£1.25p	☐
RUIN FROM THE AIR			
	Gordon Thomas & Max Morgan Witts	£1.50p	☐
DAMNATION ALLEY	Roger Zelazny	85p	☐
FALSTAFF	Robert Nye	£1.50p	☐
EBANO	Alberto Vazques-Figueroa	95p	☐
MY CHILDREN AND I	Margaret Powell	95p	☐
FIREFOX	Craig Thomas	95p	☐

All Sphere books are available at your local bookshop or newsagent, or can be ordered direct from the publisher. Just tick the titles you want and fill in the form below.

Name...

Address..

....

Write to Sphere Books, Cash Sales Department, P.O. Box 11, Falmouth, Cornwall TR10 9EN

Please enclose cheque or postal order to the value of cover price plus:

UK: 22p for the first book plus 10p per copy for each additional book ordered to a maximum charge of 82p

OVERSEAS: 30p for the first book and 10p for each additional book

BFPO and EIRE: 22p for the first book plus 10p per copy for the next 6 books, thereafter 4p per book

Sphere Books reserve the right to show new retail prices on covers which may differ from those previously advertised in the text or elsewhere, and to increase postal rates in accordance with the GPO.

(10:78)